Hard Mouth

HARD MOUTH

A Novel

AMANDA GOLDBLATT

•

COUNTERPOINT

BERKELEY, CALIFORNIA

HARD MOUTH

Copyright © 2019 by Amanda Goldblatt
First paperback edition: 2019

Library of Congress Cataloging-in-Publication Data
Names: Goldblatt, Amanda, author.
Title: Hard mouth : a novel / Amanda Goldblatt.
Description: First paperback edition. | Berkeley, California :
    Counterpoint, 2019.
Identifiers: LCCN 2018060435 | ISBN 9781640092426
Classification: LCC PS3607.O448 H37 2019 | DDC
    813/.6—dc23
LC record available at https://lccn.loc.gov/2018060435

Hardcover ISBN: 978-1-64009-327-0

Jacket design by Nicole Caputo
Book design by Wah-Ming Chang

COUNTERPOINT
2560 Ninth Street, Suite 318
Berkeley, CA 94710
www.counterpointpress.com

Printed in the United States of America
Distributed by Publishers Group West

10 9 8 7 6 5 4 3 2 1

for my family

Hard Mouth

ABBOTT: To feed a horse you take a bag and put his fodder in it.

COSTELLO: Does he stand for it?

ABBOTT: Certainly.

COSTELLO: You mean you put his father in a bag?

ABBOTT: That's right, and you hang his fodder on his nose.

COSTELLO: Now ain't that a pretty picture—a horse walking around with his father hanging on his nose!

The Abbott and Costello Show,
November 9, 1944

In this story I do not mean to hide myself. Rather I want to be obvious. I want you to see, at least, me.

Let me offer this: when I was eight I bent my mother's gold heirloom bracelet. Then I lied about it. It was an oval cuff with stamped initials: an heirloom. I pressed it against the curb in front of the house. It crushed homely. I ruined the thing. I was horrified, powerful. I hid myself beneath the kitchen window, to wait.

Ma had been watching. She came out the front door in her T-shirt with a wet spot at the stomach, had been scrubbing and standing too close to the kitchen sink. Would she ever learn to wear an apron, or to reduce the water pressure, or to stand further back? Her approximation of housewifery was then disinterested at best. Later it improved, or got worse, depending on your metrics.

Crossing the yard to get to me, Ma nearly stepped on the daffodils she'd put in the week prior. She asked me what I was doing. I was an only kid; I couldn't lay blame. I tried "on accident," "an accident," "accidentally."

"I don't know what I'm supposed to say," she said. "When you break something like this it stays broken." A hank of hair fell from her ponytail as she spoke, and affixed itself on her sweaty cheek. "Maybe your dad will have something to say. I don't."

I gave her back the ruined bracelet and she held it so that I couldn't see but a sliver of old gold between her fingers. It winked meanly. I did not wonder whose it had been. Ma left me to sit on the stoop alone, and went off to corral the moldering dinner-and-breakfast mess. Through the open windows I could hear the splashes and mutters. I didn't cry.

Rather I sat where I was, shredding a blade of grass. I watched the street. It was empty of neighbors, until a bigger kid came lumbering. "Oh hey," he said, casual in the heat. I didn't answer. I can't remember if this was Clint or Darren. At the time they were both big male kids I only heard about when Ma gossiped. The kid's basketball shorts wooshed. Years later he'd be dead from a war, or a drunk driving accident. Clint one way, Darren the other—Ma wouldn't be able to match their names with their deaths. "Does it matter?" she'd ask. In response I'd leave the room. A neighbor's death was only an abstract break-age. Ma was not interested in goodbyes, or good at them. I think of those boys not as people but as shorthand, which is probably why I remember them at all.

I watched Clint or Darren disappear beyond the hill's peak. All around me there were stripped fringes of grass. I had made a bald clearing of dirt on the lawn. I was already in trouble and so went on making my harvest. It pleased me. There is, I'd learn, some freedom in the compounding of bad behavior.

Soon Pop rolled up in the Corolla. He parked on the street as he always did—so Ma could get out later if she needed. He shuffled some heavy-sounding things in the trunk, then wrested up his briefcase, which was brown and hard sided. Pop, Dan, was tall and pleasant looking. Not celebrity handsome or catalogue handsome. Not a series regular. He had, perhaps, a kind television doctor's face. One able to communicate sincerity and compassion with his tidy professional mien. He was warm to the touch. Ma loved him and I did too. He was beloved, which is important to this story: what we'd do for him came from this attachment, and not from any drive to duty.

When Pop got to the stoop he squatted in his khakis and cheek-kissed me good, then looked at the grass. "Something going on?" he asked. I shrugged. "You coming in for lunch?" he asked. I shrugged again. I was not worried he would stop loving me but I was worried that I would be in his eyes reduced. This worry had set me silent. At the time I did not feel guilty about the bracelet, that emblem of my uncaring. He kissed me on the top of the head, said "Suit yourself, Miss Lady," went inside.

Directly I crouched under the kitchen window, to see what my parents would say to one another. But waiting, I heard only dish clinks and faucet splats. I went back to my perch, resigned, to continue my harvest. The crop was dry, green with beige papery ends that made it easy to pull one fiber from another. Soon Pop came back out and sat next to me on the step. I had missed the conspiracy. He was here to report. "Your mom's not so happy you broke her bracelet," he said. I wanted to tell him I had bent it. Though even I knew this was irrelevant.

"So," he said, "I want you to start thinking about others—about empathy." I knew the meaning of the word. I lived twenty minutes outside Washington, in an unfancy mixed-income Maryland burb of single-family homes and townhouses and apartment buildings, where culture sloughed itself unthinkingly from the downtown museums and public radio and politics. Ma and Pop had not yet given up chipping at my starchy mulishness. They could've turned to some kind of Sunday school for this, but neither had any inclination toward religion.

Pop said he had an idea. "Hop to, little one." I trotted behind him and launched into the Corolla with its living-hot leatherette seats. Once we were in motion I asked him where we were going. "To one of my properties," he said. I didn't answer. The neighbors' vinyl siding streaked into stripes as he drove.

In these early nineties there'd been a dim valley in my father's success as a real estate agent. When things got thin Ma would get a temporary job to goose us till Pop's next deal: She answered phones or filled out forms, filed or fetched, delivered or doled out. Meanwhile, when Pop's contracts ran out, properties unsold, clients would be sorry to fire him but do it anyway. Still, they liked him, and were often startled into hospitality by his charm, unfaltering in the face of his own failure. On more than one occasion, they asked us to dinner.

At these meals I don't know what adult things they discussed—the economy probably, local politics, the public schools, public art, football, golf, gossip, hunting, a new-construction strip mall up on the main road; I listened unto bleariness, then excused myself to watch TVs in dens all over the neighborhood. Once there wasn't a TV anywhere in the house and I whiled a quiet hour with nothing more than a pack of cards and a frayed finger trap. These houses were unremarkable to me as any public restroom, places to enter and use and leave.

Now we parked in a drive. He told me I could get out so I did. We were at a biggish split-level a few streets over from ours. The owners, he told me, were away tending to their daughter, who was about to have a baby. They hoped the house would be sold when they returned in a few months; it wouldn't be. Pop would've tried. For now he popped the lockbox and got the key.

It smelled clean and stale, like the library. There was wall-to-wall carpeting and a large sliding glass door by the kitchen. It went out to a cracked patio and a small, dry water feature with a fish-shaped fountain. Inside, between floors were snub flights of stairs. Our own home was a single floor rambler. These stairs were a novelty. I tested them—moving upward and downward repeatedly—as Pop, who already had plenty of empathy, let me.

After a while, longer than I'm sure I knew, my father tapped on the wall till I stopped. Then he took me up to the third floor, to the end of the hall, where the daughter's child-hood bedroom sat like a commemorative diorama. Seeing it, I imagined the couple had two versions of the same daughter: the first, grown up in the world, was about to give birth, toddling about with electric bills and fiddling with the coffee maker, and the second, who still inhabited this room, wore pig-tails and fed the dog what she did not like from her dinner.

The idea was convincing enough; the room was chock-full. It was not the neat anonymity of a parents' room, nor the pleasant gold chaos of a den with its knickknacks and junk mail. It had posters and drawings, crates of toys and stacks of paper, everything organized but not neatly, all for nobody's use. The closet door was impeded from full closure by a jumble of bags.

On the nightstand beside me, was there a framed photograph of a heavyset, beagle-eyed man in a tuxedo jacket, staring out? I can no longer remember where he was or wasn't. His presence would stitch itself across my young memory, both before and after he'd made his actual debut. More on this, later, possibly. I stood and looked at the frame, which was silverleaf, thick as a sausage or intestine.

My father told me to lay down on the bed. It had its comforter but no sheets beneath, which I discovered when I wrested the fern print quilt from its tucking. The plastic of the mattress sheath sucked lewdly against the back of my thighs where my shorts did not cover.

"Imagine you're someone else," he said, once I had settled.

"What do you mean?" I asked.

"Imagine you aren't you."

I was confused but closed my eyes and tried, because I could tell he wanted me to. Behind my eyelids I saw only black in the unlit room, blinds drawn.

"It's important that you try this now," he said. "Because this will be something good to know for the rest of your life—to know what it feels like for others, in any dealings you'll ever have with anybody."

Of course I didn't hold on to this. My guilt was a closed circuit. Long after this lesson—when I was hardly the same person, hardly the same cells—I would confirm that guilt and empathy were not comorbid. You could be guilty and careless.

You could care without comprehension or heed of blame. It was an extra step to care enough to lock empathy and guilt together such that they could drag one another forward.

I lay in the bed, eyes closed—doing my young best—while Pop said, "Now: imagine you are the little girl who lives here. This is your room. Your clothes are in that closet over there. Those are your charm bracelets on the dresser, and those are your field hockey trophies. That is your poster mapping all of the magical places in fairy tales. On it you've got a favorite toad-stool. Sometimes you dream about sitting on it.

"When I count backward from ten, you will feel yourself rais-ing out of your own body and into this little girl's." He counted. "As I hit five, you'll feel the differences. You can count them. Her eyes feel bluer. Her hair is more coarse, short like a boy's."

Now I wonder where he got this hypnosis prattle: from a professional development seminar, or a late-night infomercial, or a self-help book. It didn't matter. I was young but not gullible. I was young but aware. This was penance: I played on. My eyes and mouth were closed.

"By the time I hit two, now, you will not even remember to notice the differences. You have always had blue eyes. You have al-ways had curly hair. You have always had that scar on your knee.

"When you open your eyes, you'll simply be in your room."

At one I opened my eyes, looked around. I was still myself, in my still body. I imagined this revelation would deflate Pop. He'd be sad and quiet, in the way I hated. So I pretended the conversion had worked.

I did not look over at him for a long time. Instead politely

I chewed my cheeks. I looked at the ceiling and then, if it was there, into the photo-face of the beagle-eyed tuxedoed man in the silver, intestine-thick frame. He had an inchworm of a wrinkle between his brows and I felt very endeared to him. I considered that there might be people who I didn't know currently, who would one day be very dear to me. I worried the roof of my mouth, that interior lunar landscape. I sighed and continued this.

Soon I felt a new presence in the room. I looked up at the strange man in the doorway. He seemed pal-rich, flourishing with fondness. Instinctually, I liked him. "Do you see?" he said. I shrugged, unsure what he meant. He asked me did I want to go get ice cream.

The stillness of the house felt incorrect, unadjusted, and I found I wanted to leave it. After following him down the stairs and out of the house, I felt a bit better.

The man opened the passenger side door for me and once we were moving I lifted the seat's side lever to recline. From my new low vantage I got treetops galore, green poufs whizzing by, punctuated by dipping power lines. I yawned a bit and the man giggled under his breath and I didn't ask him why.

At Baskin-Robbins I ordered a scoop of rainbow sherbet in a cake cone. Though I knew the man across the table was my father, I couldn't stop looking at him like he was someone from history, who had lived a very long time ago. As if he were the man in the silver frame. But he was not. He was here, breathing. He did then twiddle his thumbs like someone I might've known.

Outside the ice cream parlor I asked the man if I could ask a woman with a large white poodle if I could pet it. He said yes but the woman said no, and so I merely watched it licking its ice cream cup across the sidewalk as we got into the car and rolled out of the strip mall parking lot and down the street.

When the man brought me home for dinner with his wife, she looked at me cheerily, as she set the table in a haphazard fashion. Her long hair was pulled up but not neatly. "I made your egg noodles," she said. "I'm not mad at you anymore." I didn't know what she meant by this. The woman told me to wash my hands. After first encountering a linen closet, I found a bathroom where I used extra soap. Do I see this now as some theatre I was trying? No. I was sincere and then sincere again— and courted some strangeness in doing so.

From the bathroom I retraced my steps to sit and eat the other girl's egg noodles, beside the woman and the man, at a big-leafed dining table with much more room than needed. The woman told me a story from when she was little but I couldn't concentrate on the story because the egg noodles seemed to be slightly off-color and also because it didn't seem very important. I was not then a reliable calculator of significance; I was acting on instinct and cue.

After dinner the woman led me back to the bathroom and said I should take a bath before I went to sleep. I washed myself in the strangers' soap. It smelled like flowers, and baby powder, a heavy hug. I put my face under the strange water. I peed as I let the water out, and then put a towel over my shoulders. It was pink and thin. The woman stuck her arm into the bathroom and handed me a blue flannel robe. "Here's your robe," she said, as if telling the truth.

In the cool dark of the room where I was staying, the new shadows prickled. Here there was no closet door, only the one for entering or exiting. In silhouette a freestanding wardrobe hunkered. I closed my eyes and thought of the story I had once heard about the bad girl who had ruined a family heirloom. She was very young, and silly, and didn't know what she did. It was easy to be like that at her age. Now I know it is easy to be like that at any age—easier than anything else, to be heedless. There were crickets there harping outside the window, and the sauntering light of cruising cars on the road outside. I fell asleep, and do not remember dreaming.

It wasn't until the next morning, when I woke up, that I saw my room and felt it to be mine. That I heard the fuzzy morning noises coming from down the hall and knew them to be signs of Ma and Pop. I didn't feel good or safe, and I didn't feel bad.

HERE'S AN ADDENDUM: I wrote about all this in sophomore English class, a time otherwise without catharsis, a time when I was merely battling to blot out my own angsty ruminations. It was my first explanation of being, of meaning-making. It was uneven, but heartfelt. At the time it was profitable for me to believe I'd learned my lesson. I volunteered to share it with the class.

As I read my hands shook badly in the air. Already I regretted sharing something that meant anything to me. My teacher at the time was a mom-aged woman with skin so gray it looked glue coated. After I was finished she said only: "Thank you, Denise."

We didn't like each other, or, that was what I thought then, and though I had nothing in particular against English, it was the only class I didn't share with my only friend Ken. He'd show up after, leaning against some lockers and tucking his hair behind his ears—a habit I recognized from teenagers on television. I'd shuffle out, and he'd lean and tuck and say, "How was it?" And I'd shrug and grumble and say what a bitch Ms. Landon was. I wasn't wrong, but what does that matter.

Later that day at lunch I'd asked Ken if he thought the whole walk-a-mile-in-someone-else's-shoes seemed important or dumb. He said he didn't think it was anything original, and maybe not useful either. I said "I agree," mooned up at him, plucked a fry. He was already tall, had a dirtstache, had a Buick and a permit, was new at school. We didn't go much of anywhere those first and second years of high school, when we were still learning each other. The dining car diner or the mall or the movies or a ride on the Red Line to go downtown and knock around the Mall, see what the art was up to at the Smithsonians.

We mimicked what we thought *serious* looked like, wore dark colors without committing to any particular subculture, frowned. We planned on flowering sometime later. We liked the Warhols in the basement of the Hirshhorn, the rocket pops from the snack bar beside the carousel, the Natural History's Hope Diamond, and the Beats show at the National Portrait Gallery. We liked to think about what it seemed like life could be, living as famous artists, glamorous and drunk or glamorous and hungover.

Then, one January day in my senior year, Ken dropped me off. My mother stood at the door with a plate of apple slices. The gesture was for her aberrant; I asked her what had happened, if Pop was OK. Conveying plate and daughter toward kitchen she reported that she'd heard something from a neighbor: Ms. Landon had died. It had been during an operation for a medical condition she hadn't known she'd had until things were too bleak. "It goes to show you," Ma said, "to take care of your teeth and walk between the raindrops." I got a glass of water, and chewed the apples, beginning to understand that no one had much control over what happened to them. I did not evaluate this as good or bad.

While I didn't learn empathy from the bracelet business, I did learn that I was curious about what life might do to me. Throughout my days I have learned to turn this curiosity on and off, switch-like. It's all part of my parable. Also I learned to invent what I could not feel. And finally: people and things die.

On days of particular vulnerability or boredom I wondered if in that empty house, I had become permanently split, striated—like a cooled, fat-topped broth. Or perhaps I had just learned to use it as an excuse. There would be many more separations. Bifurcations, vivisections, vacays. Many more failures in being and telling. Many more empty houses. As much emptiness as anyone could bear, and I, rushing toward it, unstopping, hardly knowing my own face.

Shifts at my first real job, I swiped in, slipped in. I tended flies in a research lab. Or, I tended the lab and sometimes the flies. I was low in the hierarchy. I tried to talk to people. I mean, I didn't try. But sometimes I opened my mouth, silently, just after they passed. I was working on the idea of being alive. It had been nearly a decade since I'd tried demonstrating catharsis in a high school classroom. Now I was an adult and didn't try things like that anymore.

Daytime was for other people. I preferred nights, their lack of friction: only then did the flies seem to take on perceptible life. As if they grew in the quiet. As if they starfished outward to make themselves known. I came to them, under lights that did not buzz. Sometimes, as if I were another person, I'd laugh. Each study had its own closet, and each hall had several closets, and I worked from one end to the other in a simple, steady pulse. This labor bloomed across my life. It could have been anything, but it was this.

The flies climbed the walls of narrow-mouthed beakers. These were closed with dense cotton plugs. The media made an immovable swamp at their bases, in which eggs hatched into larvae, pupated, then flew. A small piece of netting was held by tension, midway up, where the adult flies could rest and where the pupa could hang.

One of my tasks was to check the flies' status (alive y/n), and to prepare new beakers with new media. I made this sloggy media in batches, from an instant mix with yeast and scoops of other things, filled trayed vials, distributed, freshened. With water the media turned a coolant blue. New, it smelled lightly sweet, and old, like fruit rot. Regularly I was to tap and shimmy the adult flies from the old universe into clean new receptacles—tipping mouth of beaker to funnel and vial, up-end, let fly, tap again, stop-up—for study. If I held my ear open enough—up and back with my forefinger and thumb—I could pretend to hear them as they alighted, landed, halted, waddled. Bent over, I would watch them mount their new landscape. I'd feel a close pride. Though the glass kept me distant. I'd straighten and sigh, shake my lab coat sleeves. I could close the closet door behind me and move onto the next. When I had visited each closet, I was done.

Yet often before leaving a closet I'd feel a slow slice of grief. This feeling was inexplicable. Though I liked the idea of staying put—of setting my heart on a given genetic line, of making a home there—in the end I could not adhere. There was nothing to do in the closets besides work and look. The flies lived about six weeks, or until their use had been spent.

In light, in day, at prescribed intervals, scientists came and put the flies to sleep. They hushed them with carbon dioxide gas and shook them out onto miniature glass platforms for microscopic study. I did not like to think of this. Nor did I invest myself with the content of their studies or genius, which, I assume, often made disciplinary and sometimes national headlines and on occasion changed one person's life, or another's, or the lives of many.

After this labor I would update the supply inventory and send orders as needed. I'd set some tools into the autoclave, bend over the big sink to wash others. I'd initial the clipboard logs. I'd get myself a paper cup of watery joe from the break room. There were posters bearing reminders for several kinds of safety. There were security and emergency protocols. Infographics instructing the importance of recycling. A bulletin board declaring the latest funding awards. The fridge smelled of liquefying leftovers. The seats farted faintly for you when you sat. I'd look out across the research campus, on, to the silent whiz of the highway. There'd be one car a minute. There was comfort in this.

Night or day I was alone and alone and only sometimes lonely. I worked and went home; saw Ken and went home, saw my folks and went home; slept, showered, ate, drank, pissed, shit, went to work, and went home. Pop had once said to me: "Being a person is contributing your fair share. Being nice is doing more than that." Though I was not nice, I was a person, and so contributed my fair share. I did my best to do so inconspicuously. I negotiated myself. I was a dutiful daughter. I fetched my own dimes. I tolerated nearly everything. Days melted, one onto the next, into basins of unremarkable time.

BY THE BEGINNING of my second August at the lab I felt that at last I might be leaving my long-standing self-quarantine. I could not then say why. Now I can say that it had been at least a year since Pop had last been sick. Perhaps I was unhunching. It was summer and summer and summer, barely any air to breathe with all the water hanging there. Inside, at work, it was dim and cold. I'd started to want to greet the younger staff—ideating invitations for drinks at the bar across the street, the dew of a cold glass, unembarrassed eye contact.

I knew well enough not to try with the May-to-August college kids, who surely had their own friends and fucks, a taste of land further out than our own suburban reef. Too, the grad students were distant in their calm rigor. Though I ventured that the high school interns, so part-time they felt like hints, might be more comfortable with a crone such as myself. They would see that I was not a threat, might find me useful, the way I might bring contextual realness to their fresh fake IDs.

At last, one day—emboldened for no reason but boredom—I did approach a quiet blonde, a rising high school senior with a cartilage piercing, as she refilled her bottle from the lounge drinking fountain. I watched it fill. She screwed its top, then offered me a service industry smile. "Did you want to get in here?"

I said I did and grabbed a paper cone, filled it brim-ward. She dried the sides of the bottle with her shirt hem. "How's the summer been?" I asked, inexactly.

"Oh fine. Really busy actually." Her face flushed. "My mom's been on me to retake the SATs."

I had a gluey recollection of myself, then, at a desk in another county, filling out a scantron, nearly a decade previous.

"It'll be fine," I said. I was attempting to offer comfort as a kind of social currency.

"I know it'll be fine," she said. "Just tell my mom that."

I understood this was rhetorical. I drank my water all at once, then asked: "Do you wanna get a drink after work?" The water backed up in my throat. I sent it back down with a swallow. I reminded myself that this was not a come-on, was merely the predicate of a social life. Still I felt I might vomit on her loafers, which she wore sockless.

She made her mouth go flat. "Can't," she said.

"Wanna do it another night?"

"I don't mean to be weird, but—" She turned her whole face from me.

I nodded and went to stand in the restroom, alone, swallowing my own spit. I let the empty cone fall in the can. I wanted to give myself a boost or reminder. I could call Ken. I could quit. On the other side of the wall, in the men's, a toilet flushed. I felt pinned by my own shame till I remembered that my shift was over and I could leave. So I left.

Later, as I was unlocking my apartment door, unbuttoning my pants, ignoring the dishes in the sink, the phone rang. In my empty apartment, I waited, then answered. It was Ma calling to say: "It's back." I didn't ask questions. She requested I come over for dinner day after next. I told her I'd have to get back to her.

AT FOURTEEN I was told for the first time that my father might die. It was on a Friday. After school Ken and I had consumed a round of limp diner fries and gritty shakes, looking at one another's zits, complaining, and only half-observant that anyone else was breathing too. "So long," I'd said, when Ken stopped the car at the end of my drive. It'd been a boring day and I was glad to end it. I was looking forward to a further hermit, to snapping my bedroom door shut: a shell. To napping until it turned dark, then light again.

When I looked back from the stoop Ken gave an all-chin nod. In response I stood there then turned. His Buick puttered back down the street. The neighbors had on some loopy singsong tune, with accordions and a guitar. It ornamented the air, but when I shut the front door behind me, I could no longer hear it.

"We're in here!" Ma called, in a hoary stage-whisper.

I walked down the hall into the kitchen as I had done so often, and so unremarkably, prior. The two of them were in a dinnertime pose this midafternoon, sitting across from one another.

"Get yourself comfy," Pop said. His cheeks were luminous as brill cream. Or it must have been something in my eye. In fact I noted he was wan. There was a big bowl of oranges on the table, and next to it, the old steel juice presser and three glasses. I wondered how long they'd been waiting. "Look," he said. "Steve brought us oranges back from Fort Myers." Pop snatched one up and showed it around. "He picked them at one of those you-pick places."

"You-pick?" I said.

"Well, he-picked," Pop laughed. Then he told me to get a knife and cutting board so I did.

Ma told me to sit down. "Your father's got cancer," she said. Her face was oil and water. "It's not the bad kind."

"It's going to be some work, but we'll get there," Pop said. Ma opened her mouth and angled without a word. He patted her.

"Oh," I sighed out, feeling an imagined lung crunch. "Not the bad kind." As if Pop had said nothing. My stomach felt like what—like letting go of an inflated, untied balloon. A confused emotional flatulence. In response I began to halve the oranges, and Pop took each half and hammer-squeezed it in the device. No one was looking at anyone else. The juice dripped down, into the steel compartment at the bottom. When the compartment was full he distributed it into the glasses. The pulp congregated brightly at the surface.

We all drank the juice. The juice was bad and bitter but maybe the juice was fine and there was something wrong with my mouth; or maybe it was the dairy film of the diner milkshake curdling now. Ma and Pop slurped, uncommenting.

"I've got some errands to do," Ma said when she'd finished her juice, and stood, grabbing her purse and keys from the counter. She, deserter, hugged my shoulders and I mmhmm'd an okay.

Then it was Pop and I at the table, beside one another. I, already a monster, let him rise and wash the juice implements himself. I sat at the table unmoving until he asked did I want to watch a movie.

We settled in for three viewings back-to-back: Grant, Hepburn/Tracy, Powell. He collected old black-and-whites, mailed away for or ferreted out. He'd plucked them from the back shelves of junk shops. Pressed *record* on blank tapes during WETA's Sunday afternoons. The cassettes lived in three old fruit crates, behind the sofa in the front room where we now sat. Often, we'd watch them together.

On-screen, here's two lover ghosts perched on a fallen log, bantering beside their own sports car wreckage. Here's a roomful of fedora-wearing men bickering gruff over a missing show dog. Here's a case of mistaken identity, always a case of mistaken identity, played for laughs, or for tragedy, driving into an orchestral swell of recognition and hope. Here's people falling down dead, except it's never permanent, or else it isn't sad, or else it is, but only for one moment before strength and joy and sun prevail. Here are no flash-forwards, no bearing out the weight of bad decisions, crummily, for the rest of your life. No punished heroes, no selfish acts without instructional consequences. Rather: here is getting off scot-free, happily and neatly, over and over, with a song in your heart. The end.

These movies were glossy, speedy, poignant: nothing like me, nothing like Pop. What did we need to add to our life's inventory. With what did we vary our hearts' fare. "What's so great about these?" I'd once asked Pop. He'd smiled blankly and said, he just liked them was all. Isn't that just like a dad. This time I didn't ask him anything; we merely bolted down thirty frames a second.

At some point Ma returned but I paid no attention, riveted on the screen to the strategic exclusion of all else. The cancer would be gone by the following year, only to return as I finished up a degree at the local college, burned through two telemarketing gigs, lucked out with employment at the lab. It was not a haunting, these unruly cells dividing. Nor was it a war.

Together we watched movies. Sometimes we hugged. Life continued but I didn't think of it that way.

THE DAY FOLLOWING Ma's call I had to cover some work at the lab. I was to go in, feed the flies, and then depart. I'd return that evening for a fuller sentinel. I did not want to see the blonde rising senior. I did not want to be reminded of the minor rejection. So I delayed my departure: "Gene?" I called into my stale apartment. He did not respond. Gene was like that, so often checking out when I wished he'd check in. For an imaginary friend, he was petulant, and what I deserved. "Gene?" I called again. I was dallying. "I need a pep talk."

At last he materialized, striding from the direction of the bathroom into my little entry vestibule, already midspeech. "Why do you even try to talk to those people? They don't want ya."

I said that seemed clear.

"You gotta punch your own weight. Look for folks with open sores. The ones who can't stop crying long enough to finish up at the deli counter. Vowers of silence, of abstinence, of desperation . . ."

In the wake of Pop's first diagnosis, I'd acquired stress-related heartburn and this imaginary friend. Only the latter lingered. Gene was styled lightly, it seemed, on a failed character actor from the early twentieth century, a fat man who played sheriff and dad, judge and dupe—someone who might be on Pop's tapes. That day Gene's soft chin met a high-collared waxed canvas safari vest: Doc Livingstone by way of the studio system. "Go be a productive member of society," he barked.

"Go take a long walk offa short pier," I said back. He blew a raspberry. I laughed.

As a young child I'd had nothing like this. I'd always been with my parents or else alone, or, later, with Ken. This was the dramatic solitude of the only child, underscoring itself. In it I had been fine. But Pop's first diagnosis had pushed the envelope of fine. Gene was a way through to something else. Without him I was inert, forced to be everything I was.

"They have a saying in show business—" he began, and then did not finish his sentence. Rather he stood in his pith helmet, brim shadowing his dark brow, looking into the middle distance. I looked that way too, saw only the gummy, dusty fridge top.

Finally I asked: "What's the saying?"

"What saying?" He looked at me as if I were the imaginary one.

I let it drop.

Upon first encounter Gene had been clear and sharp, a reflective blade. He had known where to land his punches. He had known, too, how to pet me, gently enough for me to miss him when he left the room. I'm not deluded. Gene was me and not me: the right tool for the job.

But lately, it seemed Gene had been fraying, warping into nonsense more commonly. This could have been worrying, but I ignored it. "Are you coming?" I stepped outside, shut the door, locked it.

He rematerialized on the front walk and whined, "Don't rush me!" then trotted to the car.

•

THAT MORNING I took the back roads to work, the access roads and cut-through residentials. There was a long strip of road where I liked the tree-cover, which enlaced itself along a narrow park in which I had never walked. Ordinarily the shape of shadows on this route calmed me. Though on this day I had a sort of road blindness. "Will you look at that!" Gene hollered, then, too closely in my ear. He said again: "Will you look at that!"

I focused my eyes. The road was covered in dark stains. With further attention I found the stains were blood.

"Poor bastards," Gene said. "Cuts of ruined game," he said.

The road was spattered with guts for a good mile. Someone had hit a deer. Or several someones had hit several deer. There seemed enough viscera to reanimate a herd. A car going the opposite direction swerved to miss a big chunk. It was not the first time I had seen something like this. I don't know if I saw it that particular day, even. At that time, in the county, there was a deer overpopulation problem, or more accurately, a human overdevelopment problem.

"Normally, with venison, I'd say medallions, with some red wine. If you wanted to be highfalutin about it."

I looked at the ruined lives of wild things, the blood and their body parts.

"Or a saddle with currant jelly. If we can find the saddle. Maybe over there by the shoulder?"

"The shoulder of the road?" I began to feel as if my stomach was pressed beneath a seesawing weight. I wanted to run.

"Cutlets," he smacked. "With port and butter and apples and cherries. Oh yes oh yes oh yes."

I told him to shut up. In response he evaporated. I went on driving unmolested. This did not always happen, his obeying, but I was thankful when it did. My stomach eased.

ON ARRIVAL I scanned my badge and parked and walked at an average pace to the lab building without knowing what I was about to do. I was sweating but it was only the August weather. For my insides had chilled.

Inside I found the floor empty: The scientists and other techs were at a training seminar I had forgotten about or was pretending to have forgotten about. There was no evidence of the blonde rising senior, or anyone. This was thrilling to me, and I responded with a thrilling act:

I walked into the nearest closet and greeted the flies in their stopped swarms. "Hello," I breathed. I chose a beaker at random and picked it up, plucking the cotton from its mouth. The flies began slowly to rise and this thrilled me further. I continued, until every beaker in the closet was open, and then left that closet, door open, and moved onto the next, doing the same. I hit another closet, and then a fourth, and on and on until the congregating swarms were visible, freed. For the flies this was freedom, or, at minimum, escape.

Next I prepared portions of wet media on two tongue depressors, and, holding these enticements, welcomed the flies from the closets, coaxing them out into the halls. I waited patiently for the populations to converge. When the air thickened with small wings, I beckoned them past the break room, where they seemed interested in a putrescing platter of bagels.

I encouraged them forward, onward. There were better attractions ahead.

I led those flies, led them by their antennae, media voluptuously dripping across the linoleum as I walked: a Pied Piper of *Drosophila melanogaster*, humming with a lungful of busy pride. They came lilting in a soft gray cloud behind me. I walked to the end of the long, low hall, holding the security doors open. Once it seemed we were all through, I unlocked and opened the only window on the floor.

The pillowy swarm moved outward unto the open seas—I mean—the open air. However the open air was hot and heavy with water. The flies seeded themselves in. I closed the window, and did not suppress the great and happy laugh that had been building in my chest.

I'm certain they died soon after in the great, baking heat. Or would die soon, simply by nature of their encoded brevity. This liberation was gestural. I cannot deny that I used them both figuratively and strategically. I disposed of the tongue depressors, then drove the highway home in the midmorning—shift done, charges gone. I could hardly catch my breath.

Once home I sat upright on my bed and heaved. In a silk pajama set Gene lay himself beside me, blowing taunting kisses into my ear. I swear I could feel his spittle landing. At this I giggled frothily, then improvised breathing exercises to calm. In and out and imagine in your chest is a flame. In and out and soon you are blowing that flame to nothing. Gene rolled his eyes and toddled away. I breathed in and breathed out until the flame was extinguished.

Soon I greeted a thick sleep with a wooly mind. Later in the afternoon I rose and ate a large ham sandwich, along with an apple and an orange. I dressed for my night shift as if nothing had happened. My habits hadn't caught up to what I'd done. I didn't call Ma.

POP'S FIRST TIME sick, I'd been more pet than nurse, oblivious and blandly sweet. By the second time I was grown enough. In those old bad days, I'd put down my telemarketer's headset and wedge my car through rush hour, so Ma could do errands, or bathe, or breathe. Or later, when the night's lab work was done, I'd walk to my little car in the untouched calm of almost-morning, and drive the highways to a smaller road, to another, and another, until I turned down my old street. I'd park under the slim shade of the dogwoods. I'd broach the stoop, unlock the door, butting my shoulder against it to absorb the noise as it opened. I'd walk into that sleeping house, and doze on the front room couch until Ma woke me, once Pop had stirred. "The first week of treatment makes you feel strange," Pop had said in those days, "and the second week you feel powerful, and the third you're too tired to raise your arms." He'd stayed tired for months after, the second cancer's long slog. Often after that first stir, he'd return to sleep, thinly, through the morning.

Pop would start his days with some applesauce, in which Ma or I would mix a phantasm of powders and drops. These are the things he would take, at various junctures, in various combinations: Vitamin D, selenium, melatonin, l-glutamine, rosemary, ginger, holy basil, hu zhang, skullcap, golden thread, oregano, barbary, and B12. The results were vivid brown, looking more compost than comestible. Many of these were Ma's own ideas, internet culled or overheard in a waiting room. I added flaxseed meal or fish oil or psyllium husk, when his intestines were uncooperative. The oncologist liked to joke that even his old Chinese mother didn't take as many herbs—he advised against garlic, green tea extract, reishi. We tried yogurt, once, instead of applesauce, but the powders stuck to themselves in dry pockets that even a man with no appetite could call unsavory. It all went into a blue bowl. I liked to put the bowl on the white wicker breakfast tray with the glass top. Surely there were better ways to try to live, or die.

Carrying the tray I'd open the door with a strict click, and never look directly at him. Once the tray was on the floor, I'd open the venetian blinds with their demure metallic shuffle. I'd look at the shallow bowl of pennies on the dresser. The mail stack. Library books—action, cinema history, American industry, the things he loved—were in several piles, their plastic covers creased, casting dull light. An orange clot of prescription bottles covered entirely a small table. There was a tablecloth over the television. And there in my periphery would be my father, under a thin sheet sweating. I'd sit on the chair in the corner, performing a tolerant, nurturing pose. Sickness had dismantled some of him, and the companion depression more, the way it can with every body.

"Guts are what you better look out for," Ma said often. "The thorax in general. Your father's family has a history." This moment pressed down insistently, a doorbell drone.

Often Pop wouldn't rouse before I left the room. Nor would I rouse him. I'd only sit with his thickening, sweetening decay. Ma preferred that I be present, if not permanently then consistently; should he wake I could feed him. Here I courted my own lessness, watching his wan, sylphy body overwhelmed. Later I'd leave the room, a solemn deboarding sailor. Ma would come later, if needed, to feed him the applesauce, after her nap in my old bed. I'd take care of the dishes or fold the laundry, check in about prescriptions and appointments and insurance, and say goodbye. The routine, its memory, unfurled, stained, pinned. But it did not stay like this.

One autumn—after years of this second sick bed, of chemo, of radiation, of applesauce—Pop had surgery. After the surgery, he got a colostomy bag. It was beige, the color of a Band-Aid. I saw it only once. Technically he was fine to leave the house but he didn't return to his daily swim. He hardly spoke, as if practicing for death. Half-conscious, we watched his old movies. They went unabsorbed, their scores simply brocading the still house. I couldn't tell you the plot of a single one.

Pop's self-concealment lasted a season, and only ceased when Ma cheered him out the door. We drove to the medical center in Baltimore, passing the football stadium and the baseball stadium and cutting through downtown, into the row house neighborhoods and boulevard parks full of adults, kids cutting school. "Whatever it is—" Ma started to say. I tapped the passenger side window and Pop tapped back. We parked in the garage, took the elevator, signed in, sat. Then we got called.

The patient, the doc noted, was relatively young and fit, and

the surgery had gone well. There was no more evidence of cancer, which made it more than remission, Ma would say later,
back in the car. It was "remission, plus!" Her optimism made
me worry. Later a surgeon repaired Pop's intestines. The repa-
ration broke his thick sulk: He chortled at being "made whole."

I remembered, how, during the first all clear, we'd eaten crabs
and made toasts about health and strength on an Eastern Shore
dock where it smelled of gas and sweat. But this time, we'd had
no celebration. We were no longer foolish this way. Or, we slept
deeply, on nights we lucked out. This was celebration enough.

I never thought we'd gotten off scot-free. At the clearance
rack in a mall store, stopped at a red light—I'd remember what
could happen, and the threat of an impending crash would fill
my ears like static. I'd have to sit down, excuse myself, pull over.

THE FLIES WERE flying free but the drive back to work was
plain and straight. I took the highway, in the direction counter
to the rush hour. I parked the car and walked across the campus.

In the lobby of my building stood a principal investigator,
huffing. He was one man or another. I felt it was unnecessary to
divine his expression, to sort nonverbal cues. I listened only, as
he explained that I'd need to surrender my badge directly. The
security tapes had revealed, he said, "all you've done."

The PI, was, while speaking, swatting flies. It seemed that
some had elected to stick to the interior. They winked in and
out of visibility. I gave them a slight, congenial nod that seemed
to confuse the man. He told me he wouldn't pursue charges
only because the bulk of the flies were at life cycle's end and held

no important data. But this was untrue—it was a kindness, or a disinclination to make a "thing" about it, or both.

As I was walking to HR for my exit forms Ma called again but I ignored her. Gene was side-trotting beside me, cheering. "Huzzah! Huzzah! The hero is at last a victor!" I pushed down my smile for appearances. I didn't worry then, but Gene's laud was never a good sign. He loved chaos, and hedonism, and shooting things.

All through the HR process I kept my mouth shut. Soon enough I was back in the parking lot, standing next to my car. I wondered if I would cry. Instead I found myself laughing again. The asphalt steamed hotly as if mad. It was later afternoon and all around me everyone was leaving, getting in their cars, pulling out, going away. Gene punched me brotherly in the arm. "What're you gonna do with this stretch of open road?" he panted. When I told him to go away he did, as if I'd earned his obedience with my misdeed.

For my next trick I decided to be a regular person. By that I mean I decided to get drunk. First I had to clear the decks for action. Sitting in the car with the windows down, I called Ma. "Where've you been?" she asked. "Will you come to dinner? Tonight? Tomorrow?"

I told her tomorrow, got off the phone quickly. For a moment I joshed myself, thinking I'd collar a newly exed colleague on their way out. Wait for an intern to leave for the day; beeline to a college kid; hunt for a drinking buddy. Be aggressive about it. Stop them on their way to the fully loaded Geo Metro, the parent's Beemer, the beater wagon. Wait, and then pounce.

But I didn't feel like talking to anyone who knew me. Or who knew who I'd presented myself to be. So I rolled out of the parking lot and through its gate, knowing there was no access to return. I didn't care.

Across the four-lane road there was a tony apartment complex where many of the brilliant young scientists lived, the ones without families, the ones without requirements for a yard. The ones who liked to get a happy hour cocktail, or watch a sports game in public. Because of this there was a bar off the lobby, a perfectly clean establishment, a correct target. I parked in the visitor lot.

Walking to the bar in the hot air, I could feel a sour brightness on my tongue. As if the gin had already hit. Inside I found an icy AC wind and a bleary Friday crowd. I sat down and ordered my cocktail, felt pleased with myself for sitting upright, gulped.

It felt fun—I'll admit—to be there, tipsy, rather than sober in the lab building, hushing around in my white coat and only half-concerned with what my body was doing. There was now very little left for me to care about, beyond the obvious. I shredded my beverage napkin with precision. I smirked at nothing. I tugged at my cotton-blend office wear, until I could remember the skin beneath. I drank.

Two drinks in, a conventionally handsome blonde man approached. I clocked him to be undangerous. When he smiled by way of introduction, his eye-twinkle was age sharpened. He reported he was waiting for some friends, who were late, and did I mind if he sat beside me? "I've been looking, and you're the only non-nerd here," he said.

"If you only knew the half of it." I gestured to the barkeep for another. I wondered what made me stick out. Fair, I wasn't wearing one article of performance clothing. I didn't have the muscle tone of weekender charity runs. I didn't have a gloss of promise in my eyes. He gave me his name, but I didn't listen. He said he was a lobbyist on the Hill, and Hill is what I called him. He asked what I did.

"Hill!" I said. "Hill, I work in a genetics lab across the street." I took a slug of my drink. "I mean, I worked in a genetics lab across the street."

He whiffed by the tense correction, asking, "What kind of work does that entail?"

"I work with flies," I said, grinning. *"Drosophila melanogaster."* Thinking of the flies was enough to make me moon. As was his unremarkably attractive face. Touching the smooth knit of Hill's trousers, I thought, this is the way damaged adults stop short of offing themselves: inaccurate conversations with strangers, mild obliteration, small criminal acts.

Previously I'd had very little capacity for intrigue or drama. Ask Ken to confirm and he'd start to snore. In this condition, in this bar, I was willing to change. To make a minor move. It was necessary. Or it seemed that way. It would require the heavy lifting of getting more drunk. I'm not of mutable stock. Or, it takes a lot to get this big, boring boulder rolling.

"At this point," I purred, "we're just crunching preexisting data." It was a small thing to do an impression like this. On his own trip, Hill was paying attention to the way my mouth moved. People of all ages and experience are familiar with this. For self-omission, objectification has its use.

I watched Hill click the mouth of his beer bottle against his neat square teeth, wondered who he was. I imagined he was three months out from a major heartbreak, a triathlete ex-girlfriend recently relocated to a minor Midwestern city to head up grassroots for a sure-thing campaign. Both were too pragmatic for long distance. He was trying to devote more time to self-improvement and to friends, to putting himself out there. There was nothing to base this on, except that he was a white man with clean clothes and good teeth, out and catting around.

"You from here? You sound like it."

"Ugh, no," I said, like some real young person, then lied: "I'm from outside Cleveland."

"Go Buckeyes?"

"Sure. You?"

"New York."

"The city?"

"Westchester. Ossining."

"Sing Sing?"

"Don't hold it against me."

"How does it go? 'Only if you ask me to'?" Then I laughed quickly, to show I must be joking, while simultaneously suggesting the option of our bodies meeting this way. Loosely I slid my drink back and forth on the bar in front of me. My body was all overlubricated joints. Hill pecked me on the cheek. As if the kiss were an award for being there, beside him.

Looking down I saw I had spilt my drink and dragged an arc of liquor like a comet's tail across the bar. I wondered if I would make my exit—call a cab, or cross my fingers and drive. Surely I would not lead myself further in. Was I wholly inexperienced? I was not. However I didn't want to make a connection while so interested in the reverse.

But funny how logic leaves, for then in a cloud of charisma came Hill's friends. It was hard to keep track of myself in their airy camaraderie. Monica—pretty, thick bangs, a sharp chin—was in epidemiology at the research institution of my previous employ, and Omar—appealingly boyish in an after-hours rugby shirt—there in gerontology. Both worked far across the campus from my former lab. Surely news of my fly liberation would not have traveled that far, that quickly. There was no sign or utterance that it had.

While it was still happy hour, I covered a round. I watched and listened to these people, these friends. I made small, bad jokes; they laughed. We drank until we were more liquid than solid. At one point I looked into the mirror behind the bar, beyond the neat rows of sleek bottles. My face was luxuriously blank, a bowl; I could pour anything in. I felt an opening in my chest, which then fractured coldly: Gene's punim was there beside me, grumpy and crimped. "Fake," he mouthed theatrically. "Fake," his lips curling. I shut my eyes, and took the shot I was given. For now I was theirs, and not his.

At nine there was chittering about changing venues, going upstairs to Omar's condo. Where the trio marched, I was their little dog. Pay the tab; get vertical; stay vertical; cross the lobby; board the elevator; press a button; rise.

•

THE ELEVATOR DOORS opened with a confidential whoosh. Seeing Omar's crisp condo, I nodded, unrealized expectations met. Danish modern furniture. Colonialist-imported gewgaws. The finishes: chrome and polished glass. The lights: strung from suspended beams and twinkling.

Out the living room window was a view of the research campus—within it acres of top-notch education, soup smells in the break rooms, shoes worn down while no one was looking, telephone détentes about budgets, bringing good science to good people for the greater good—and beyond that, the gleaming highway with its constant loop of shooting cars, headlights on— one strip gold, the other taillight red—then even farther out, the pebbled barrier walls, the tops of trees; and above all a red cloud ceiling hanging low with light pollution, convex somehow, a heavenly belly. I was not used to being up so high. My father, who had always felt irritable in apartment buildings for professional reasons, preferred his sweeping views from the top of the Washington Monument or similar. Let home be simple, for resting your sleepy head, he'd say. Let me go out, into the world, to see such a view! Never mind the windows in the Monument were small, and made everything look like a dollhouse oil painting.

I saw I had crossed the apartment and was standing against the glass. From behind me Omar asked gently did I want a drink. I said yes. He was an ideal host—a charming, harmless flirt, a flatterer, a profferer, a light ribber. It was a momentary feint of pleasure. I dined upon it, unready to digest.

Soon I found myself propped against the kitchen island, between the host and Hill, who fiddled with a dime. Monica was sitting in a loveseat beneath a pendant lamp in the corner, dangling a shoe from her foot: The lamp lit her up, how lit she was, how lit we all were. Omar poured expensive clear liquor over clear-eyed ice into heavy tumblers. I tittered and forgot cancer. I swilled and forgot my blousy trash bag of a pal.

When I think about this night, it is grossly and glamorously shellacked with the intoxication of belonging. It marked the beginning of an era of habit: to act outside of what felt comfortable.

One moment I felt sober and the next, soused. The walls seemed to corset me. "I'm so sorry," I said. "I can't. I really apologize." I didn't know what I was apologizing for. Had I been drugged? No. Hill said something to me, then Monica. Omar's body stiffened into a truss. Monica kicked off her other shoe. The three friends united to support me, my tipping body. One of them held my wrist in three fingers. And, as I lay down, that wrist was placed at my side, my self a rock thrown and sinking into the center of a deep stream. In fact I was on the couch. There I did my best to calm the current of my vision, my claustrophobia, my sweat, my alcoholic nausea.

When all had calmed and cooled, an hour or more passed, I got up and crossed the room.

"Oh, it's our coma patient," Monica said, from where she sat on the kitchen island, her legs open and Omar leaning between them. I wondered what I had missed.

"You're just in time," Hill said, holding out a glass of water. I wondered was it Kool-Aid, Jonestown-style. Fine, I thought. OK, I thought.

Of course it was only water. "How are you feeling?" Monica

asked. What time was it. Outside I saw a watery dark. There were no taillights or headlights on the highway anymore, or, then, just one or two cars whizzing like mites. I felt sawed in half, a breeze between. I smiled to show I was fine; I stopped midway between the living area and kitchen, turned, found the nearest chair, something upholstered, and landed.

All three new friends rotated toward me from the kitchen island. Hill, Omar, Monica. They patted one another encouragingly. They continued to gulp the hooch. The lucky lived at a different tempo. I was unlucky but not unluckiest. I merely lived slow, under the reeking pendulum of death. In their company I saw how this had marked me. I attempted to refocus my vision. I was still drunk.

Had I been able to choose the follow-up event from a menu of the two biggest options—sex, death—I would have surely chosen sex: something redolent of the seventies and future both.

But though the set was primed for hedons, I, still recovering, sat on my hands literally. This inaction seemed to drive the lovely night into a crater I would not for some time leave. If it is not sex, it is death. If not quickly, then eventually.

"Are you okay, Denise?" asked Hill. "Drink your water."

I noted the glass, which had appeared in my hand, and obeyed. He had left the kitchen island to approach me. Upon his arrival he stroked my hair. I liquidated.

"I want a pizza," Monica announced. She slapped the island in emphasis.

"You don't," Omar said. "You want some nice endive or carrots or some kale."

"The more you look at the aged, the more it seems like a crapshoot," Monica said.

"It doesn't matter what you do, right? We're all fucked."

"So why do you run marathons?" Hill asked Monica, winking at me. I had forgotten I was in the room.

"Because, I'll tell you why." Monica raised her glass. "Because I drink enough to pickle my fascia back to front."

"I'm not sure it's possible to pickle collagen," Hill said, then addressed me: "I was premed for a couple years . . . No, it must be. Pickled pigs' feet. Hooves and all."

Omar was then bent into the open fridge, ravaging his crisper. "I have carrots with the tops still on, the aforementioned kale, a few asparagus spears . . ."

"I want none of those," Monica responded. "I would like most in the world to have pizza."

"Pizza, okay, if not nutrition, then, think of the carbon footprint. Delivery." I noted Hill was fucking with her. "One round trip of emissions for one meal for one person?"

"I was going to share."

"It's tragic," Omar added.

I thought to myself that it was not tragic. Or: it was not tragic yet. That was the point of climate change—so sluggish then that we wouldn't care as much as we should've. Later would come fires, floods, displacement, condo towers built on the coast of Florida with insufficient accommodations for the sea level's rise—it seemed my grog was evaporating. I had a feeling, en route to a waking, warm nausea, that I had once been intelligent. That feeling was a scam.

I was doing my best to keep body and soul together. That was Pop's saying, something he'd rustled up somewhere when he was first sick, a homily in response to any inquiry. "Working on keeping body and soul together." All at once he'd started saying it, and then it was there forever: an unretractable obelisk pricking up from the formerly peaceful ground.

Omar sat on the floor with his kale, waving it like a victorious Olympian. Everyone laughed, even me. He scrabbled up from the floor with Hill for leverage.

"All of our decisions mean something," he declared. Monica snorted and came to sit in the chair beside me.

"Can you go through life worrying about all that?" I asked. "Doesn't it get tiresome?"

"A cynical geneticist," Hill said. "Fascinating."

"It's not that fascinating," Omar said. "You only start out being idealistic. Idealism is directional toward cynicism necessarily."

"Genes, or any inherited thing, are destiny, if anything's destiny," I said flatly.

"You're completely right," said Omar. "Especially when it comes to certain samples of the population, certain ethnicities and predispositions combined with systemic—medical even—oppressions—"

"Then what was with the kale just now?" Hill interrupted.

I didn't want Hill to have interrupted Omar because what Omar had been saying was interesting. All night it had been babble. In not knowing anything else this had been adequate. But now Omar returned to babble, relubricating, sighing, answering: "Habit."

"Halibut!" Monica piped from the loveseat, giggling. She slid from the chair down to the floor. Omar found a bower beside her.

"That's depressing," he said.

"I read a thing that half the time when you think you're ordering one kind of fish at a restaurant it's another," Omar said.

"Yeah," Monica said. "I read that too."

"Overfishing!" Omar said.

"What do you work on again?" I asked Hill. It was unclear if we had covered this.

He told me nuclear nonproliferation. He told me "liaison between analysts and politicians."

"He's the good kind of lobbyist," Monica said, in a confidential way that made me feel like they must've slept together at some point.

"That why we keep him around," Omar added.

"How's it going?"

"How's what going?"

"The proliferation or non-, or—"

"Eh," Hill shrugged and winked again. He was an overeager winker. It was not endearing.

"What do you mean, 'eh'?" I asked.

"I mean, you win some, you lose some."

"Do you know ahead of time, before the winning and the losing?"

"My job is to tell the politicians. The whiches and whens are for the analysts."

"How do they figure it out?"

"It's a combination of number crunching and game theory, or, I don't know—strategy."

"Are they right much?" I asked.

"They're right enough to keep their jobs," Omar said.

"Sure, they're right enough. But numbers don't control sociopolitical forces. They just predict their movements and produce probability," Hill offered blearily, rotely, as if he were making small talk about a football game.

"Why can't they control it?" I asked. I didn't mean to ask this.

"They get out of control sometimes. The empire is imperfect," said Omar.

"Like what?"

"North Korea, obviously. India and Pakistan and Russia for some others. To say nothing of Iraq and cakes of whatever, a few Japanese fatalities—" Omar offered.

"The Japanese fatalities were an energy issue. Not an arms issue. And so not really my fault," said Hill.

"Whose fault was it then, God's?" Omar asked.

Hill was silent for a moment, gob-stopped, cheek-slapped, silently gulping, and then: "God's?"

We all took turns looking stunned. Then guffawed. The inaugural meeting of the Friday Night Atheists was going swimmingly.

"Let me pose a question then," Omar said, moving from the floor into the chair above. He began to give Monica a neck rub. "Probability, Mark, that the world will end as a result of us blowing it up?"

"Statistically, or in my opinion?"

"In your expert opinion."

"Goddamn small."

"But it would only take a button or two, wouldn't it?"

"Yes, in one model. But the Cold War is over. We're all too scared, it turns out, to push the buttons. Or if at some point it turns out we aren't, it's too late to save us all anyway, and we deserve what's coming."

"Yowza, Mark. What about the chance of an accident with a computer?"

"Microscopic."

"Terrorists? Robots?"

"I don't know. Maybe. Outside of my purview."

"Then how do you propose the world will end?"

"Slowly, and painfully, and while hardly anyone in this country is watching."

At this Monica disengaged her neck from Omar's hands, flattened herself to the rug. "Must you be so awful all the time?"

"No, but I like to be." Then Hill winked at me once again, and pulled me down to the rug beside him. I ventured it was one wink too far. He had clean nails. I'd noticed this earlier as he'd picked through a tech magazine on the counter. His lunulas were white as a gallery wall. I imagined what it would be like to spend an afternoon with him. I wondered if he would at some point stop winking. I tugged his collar, just to see what it felt like, and when he jumped, he gave me a funny little look I couldn't decode. I felt tired again.

"I feel tired," I announced.

For the first time that night all the strangers looked like

strangers. I'd interrupted their fun. "Drink your water," the closest stranger said. My glass remained full as it had ever been.

"Go lay down," the lady stranger said. "It's late."

An angry flush swept my cheeks. At last I drank the water. I got up and walked over to the sectional. If you like to be liked, a new friend can make you feel immortal. If you don't, the whole thing is exhausting. "You know what scares me?" said one stranger. "Gray goo." I made my body horizontal. I closed my eyes.

"See, that's what I'm talking about," said another. "Nanotechnology could easily get away from us."

"Trillions of infinitesimally small monsters, invisible to the human eye, invading us cell by cell . . ."

In the last little dregs of waking, I thought how I did not fear an end to the world as I knew it, the way these people did; for I did not know much of the world, and what I did know I did not connect with joy. I was filled to the brim with dread; it threatened to spill blackly from my mouth.

THAT NIGHT, I fell asleep on Omar's couch. Later I woke to Hill's insistent finger petting my neck. I pretended sleep until the finger retreated. When later I opened my eyes I was sure I could see Gene's silhouette against the window. Hitchcock sans elegance. I ignored him. Yet there he stood as I allowed Hill to advance. I did not think I liked to be watched but couldn't see another way.

"Finally," Hill breathed into my ear. "I can't believe how long that all took."

"Men must learn to be patient," I said to Hill and Gene. Gene, for his own sake, turned away.

Here Hill had been waiting. I had not been waiting, just living. Now I was half-asleep. What did he think of me, I wondered, looking over at Gene's broad back. What did I think of me. Did it matter? I was raw with this.

I wondered what it must be like to be another person. I then remembered how people have bodies, and how these bodies, that people have, work in such fascinating configurations. Here, a flash of sexual excitement.

Hill lifted my ass and put his knee between my thighs. "Hello," he said. "Is this okay?" A wrapped condom flashed dimly between his fingers.

"Yeah," I said. "Of course." I looked back over to Gene but he was no longer there.

I stripped from the waist down. Hill pressed into me. His khaki pants rubbed against the summer dry skin of my legs. They made a slight scraping sound, like Velcro peeling from itself.

AFTER, I FELL asleep. When the sun cut over the research campus I cracked my eyes open and rose. There were some withering greens, a couple of empty bottles, Monica's shoes, tipped: each object a body unto itself. Hill was down beside the couch. From above I looked at his clean, clear face. Then he opened his eyes and we smiled together. He got up. His arm, an intimate hook, tried to pull me back down. He told me I should stay a while.

I left. I walked down the hall. The elevator doors whooshed.

I was carried downward thinking: goodbye forever you new friends.

I SPENT THE next day vomiting into the toilet, and drinking water. The bathroom linoleum was sticky with my kneeling sweat. As I let loose my bucketfuls of bile, I thought I could hear Gene through the bathroom door, cackling till he coughed. "Get!" I shouted, acid hoarse. If he had answered he might have said: If you can't handle a tipple, then you may best abstain. Instead the laughing stopped.

I was glad for it. Often Gene was the quicksand I found myself in, or the air I wished I couldn't breathe. I thanked myself for small favors and resumed my retch. Later I let the shower beat my skin, and dried in the cutting breeze of central air.

That evening, still clouded, I drove from my far-flung part of the county—that rural land prickling with new construction— to my folks' denser burb. The highway was newly paved. Still my sedan shuddered once I hit sixty. In response I said to it: "I know how you feel."

I was trying to figure out whether I would tell my parents about my dismissal. I decided to stay mum. As I parked on the street I noticed the rosebush leaves were pus yellow. I went on walking.

In the kitchen the takeout was already on the table, carton flaps bouncing slightly under the ceiling fan's agitation. Ma greeted me with the usual pose: arms out, a flattening hug. She was trim; no, she was gaunt; no, she was simply always *skinnier*.

"Where's Ken?" I asked. I saw that Pop was propped at the

end of the table, two pillows behind him. "What is this, Passover?" He seemed to be courting invalidity. It made me mad.

"Your father wanted a little extra," Ma said.

"Where's Ken?" I asked again.

"I sent him out for some ice cream."

"You want anything to drink?" I asked Pop from the kitchen, my head in the empty larder. "You guys have some grocery shopping to do."

"He's got some of that ginger tea going," Ma said.

"I was asking Pop," I said.

"Get some serving spoons?"

I dug my fingers between the spoons in the silverware drawer. They clicked together in a way I did not like.

"Will you do me a favor, while you're here?"

I nodded. Ma's hair was frizzed into a halo; she wore saggy pants covered in flour or powder or soap. She took both of my hands and made me look at her in her sad, thinning face. We did a little sidestep so that we were standing like solemn dance partners in the doorway between the kitchen and hall. "Denise," she began. "I need to go over some documents with you, for the hospital, and for after." The house was overcold; I was in need of an overcoat. Or anything that could hide me.

"I'd prefer not to talk right this moment?" I asked. Or simply said it.

Then the front door opened and behind it was Ken. The hot day came with him. His shopping bag crackled; his hello warmed me up. "Hey beautiful," he said, and kissed me on the head.

"Chocolate-chocolate chip?" I asked.

Ma kissed Ken's cheek to formalize the favor done. I will admit to having a hot dense feeling in my shoulders, then. Because he was not my mother's child he could pretend to take joy in service. Or perhaps he was sincere.

"Can you tell?" I whispered into his ear, as we sat down at the table to eat. I sniffed. "Do I smell like eighty proof?"

"It's okay to not be okay." He hugged my head into his solid chest like I was a dog. I wondered how he already knew.

An alcoholic vapor did seem to be issuing from my poor pores. I couldn't tell if he was listening to me. The house had been overtaken by the food's garlicky savor. The cartons crowded on a lazy Susan. I sat down at the dining table, between Pop and Ken. Ken sat next to Ma. Then there was a chair, then there at the end of the table, again, was Pop. I imagined us as clock hatches. We began spooning food onto plates.

Pop reached his hand over to mine. "Hey honey," he said. In his other hand was a balled-up napkin.

"Hey Pop," I said, and opened the box of crab Rangoon to give him one. "Veggies?" I asked. They were in a white sauce, all cornstarch and salt and sugar, lascivious pea pods and suspect shoots. Pop demurred.

I turned up from the food and hung the vegetable carton in the air. "Anyone?"

Ken took it and I took my own crab Rangoon and began to snap its pastry corners. It tasted like a fryer with a tang of factory-by-the-sea.

"Will you move Pop's tea closer to him?" Ma asked.

"I hate it when you call him *Pop*," I said. "Just call him Dan like everyone else. And he should call you *Marilyn*, never *Ma*."

"Okay, fine, will you move Dan's tea?"

"Don't give your parents such a hard time," Ken said. I made a loopy comedienne face and went back to my Rangoon.

"Is that all you're eating?" Ma asked. I clipped my chin at her own empty plate. "What? I'm old. My stomach is small." I told her that was dumb.

There was too much food on the table. It disgusted me: the vegetables and the Rangoon, scallops and string beans and General Tso's chicken, sweet-and-sour and egg drop, four luck pork and shrimp lo mein, craggy platters of rice. I pushed the lazy Susan around and around until Ken told me to stop because I was making him seasick.

I got up for a glass of water. When I looked through the kitchen window into the front yard, I saw the brush grass and, beyond, one-stories with carports, both sides of the street all parked up with dinged SUVs and shitty sedans. Like a scene from a movie or dream I recalled then the view from Omar's condo: the highway, its distant motoring mutter. I was back on the ground floor now.

When I tuned back in I saw that Ma had at last taken some vegetable fried rice. Everyone was chewing, even Pop. With a pained face he was chewing, and swallowing, too.

"How's work?" Ma asked Ken.

"Usual. I got some new supervisor, the manager's kid. He's nice but he doesn't know how to work with people."

"Maybe he should just work with flies, like Denise," Ma said.

I stuck out my tongue, even though it had chewed wonton wrapper on it.

"Denise, close your mouth!" Ma said. Then she laughed.

"It's the see-food diet," I said. I was doing a reenactment of a movie I'd seen once.

From the end of the table, Pop began to guffaw. It was an industrial noise. His body, in those days, never seemed to have enough moisture.

"Easy, Dan," Ma said.

"Let him laugh at my funny joke," I said.

"If it was funny, maybe," Ken said. He got up and got Pop a glass of water. Pop patted his arm, and then we were all sitting again, chewing again, except Pop. We all noticed.

"Pop has something to tell you guys," Ma said, nearly formally.

"You mean Dan," I said.

"Pop has something to tell you guys," she said.

We all looked at the gray man at the end of the table, propped up on his pillows. He was only at the end of his fifties, but brittle looking, everywhere except his eyes: that firm soft stare wouldn't yet quit.

"Denny," Pop spoke. "Ken. I'm not getting any treatment this time. We're just going to let everything take its course."

I imagined then a large boulder, lobbed off a quarry cliff, into a bottomless depth of water. Someone had muted the scene. I searched and saw Ma, still, with her mouth open slightly, caught between rest and action. Ken was already up, hugging Pop at his seat. I got up too. I hugged too. One or fifty minutes later Ma was there. Soon we were all hugging each other, in the still-bright light of an August evening, in some room among other rooms, in some house among other houses, in some suburb among other suburbs, in some metropolitan area in some state, along other states, along the rest of the country, along its countless peopled features.

Some think this is what love feels like: this quick stomach drop, this timeless, hazy drowse. They're wrong. This is the beginning of loss. How does a moment like this end? I found my face wet. Someone else was crying also. Or maybe it was only the other person crying. I opened my eyes but saw only shadowed limbs and torsos abstracted. I shut my eyes again and imagined the boulder at the bottom of the quarry water, having hit rocky sand, settling in.

Ken, our fine unrelated familiar, was the first to speak. "We all support you, Dan," he said. "If it seems like the right thing to do, then we support you." His words were muffled in our hug.

At last we all straightened up. Ken sat back down and Ma sat back down and I kneeled beside Pop. Though already I was returning to my scalding self, apart from this intimacy. Soon those who had been eating were eating again. The grit on the floor bit into my knees. I sunk into a cross-legged position, and fished for the rest of my crab Rangoon like I was getting something off a high shelf. I chewed it slowly beside Pop's leg. He petted me. I chewed the Rangoon into a salty paste, then found a napkin to spit it out. The paste was faintly pink. Later in bed

I would discover with my tongue the shreds of my cheek's interior, which I had been chewing unthoughtfully along with the dumpling.

Soon enough the meal was over and Pop was escorted by Ken to bed. Ma started with the dishes.

"You're going to have to take the leftovers if Marilyn doesn't want them," Ken announced when he returned to the kitchen. The table was wrecked with grease.

"I won't even eat them though," I protested. "Take them."

"I sure as hell don't want them," said Ma, clattering over the dishwasher.

I asked Ken why couldn't he take them. With my fingers I calipered his side. "You should eat!"

"So what have you been doing with yourself, Denise?" Ma asked. She held out a saucer of fortune cookies in their merry cellophane. She changed the subject anytime she liked.

"The usual," I said. I didn't want to take a fortune cookie so I didn't. It was difficult to understand what I was doing there, anymore. No one had touched the ice cream. The carton gave off a thin pool of water.

Ken said he had to go. Ma walked him to the door and as they embraced I fooled with the ice cream defrost pool, drawing spokes or spikes outward from the carton, remembered the dragged arc of liquor on the bar. Ken called goodbye from the front room. I hollered back in kind.

Ma came back with lips so pursed they seemed to disturb the air. "Denise! You're making a mess."

"It's just water."

She found a rag and sopped my spokes. "We don't have to talk about it tonight."

"Okay." I introduced my hands to one another, twiddled my thumbs.

"But if you want to."

"Okay."

"It's just another decision," she said. "How long is this supposed to go on?" She put the ice cream in the freezer.

I made a sound with a closed mouth. Through the kitchen window I could see Ken's car drawing itself out of the scene. The sun was back behind the neighbors' houses, lighting them up at the edges. Our house was growing dimmer and dimmer. I don't mean to make this so plain. Perhaps the drama was undercut by Ma washing dishes. I wished I was washing dishes. Just then I ached for so minor a duty.

Down the street and into moderate traffic, I drove home the long way—through the old horse fields built over with single-family homes and their two-car garages; next past a church, and another church. Gene was nice enough to sit shotgun; I was glad for the company. Just anything might've done: a crash test dummy or mall mannequin. I imagined him stroking my jaw with his thumb but actually he was just looking out at the streets, counting mailboxes and humming to himself. "What do you think about all of this?" I asked. He didn't say a thing.

At a stop sign I turned to look at him, my quivering behemoth. His hair was steely and parted and pomaded neatly, his lips thick, his ventriloquist dummy chin giving way to a thoracic spread. His eyes a sparkly bit of rodentia. The setup made me swoon, with companionship or thanks.

I know: Gene was there and not. Like faith, or air. I only believe in one of those things, but—he was a modern convenience, a thing that you could use unthinking, on most days.

"Well?" I asked again, moving through night neighborhoods.

"Oh I don't know. Don't rush me," he croaked, rubbing his knees back and forth in an agitated way. He wore shirtsleeves and braces. The pits of the shirt were wetted dark; the sleeves stretched around his hairy arms. "These kinds of things take a lil' time to turn over." His wattle wavered with him. "Oh well. Well, I don't know. Well! I guess every man's gotta go sometime." He blew his nose into an apparitional handkerchief and tried again: "It's like this: once, when I was at a card game with Cary, he asked me did I want to talk real talk."

"Who, Cary Grant?"

"Oh, you know him?"

"You don't, didn't."

"I did," he brooked. "At least when I was alive!"

It was a going routine that he had once been a real person. I couldn't decide if he was a liar, or believed himself to be telling the truth. Either way I was a secret sucker for my own tall tales. Sometimes he was a hero fighter pilot and sometimes he was a movie star and sometimes he was a great explorer. Sometimes just a person, unnotable as I. In conjuring Gene I was undependable: unreliable or forgetful, or both. I went on driving, humoring my man. "You didn't," I said, smiling awfully. I yielded for two teens shrugging across the way.

"Does it matter? Will you listen?"

"Maybe I'll listen." I turned off the AC and let in the cool night air. We were rolling through quiet streets hazy with the coronas of sodium lamps. A house, a house, a long stretch of dirt. In my part of the county cow pastures were in the midst of obliteration, construction, development—a remaking by the busy, unminding hands of capitalism.

"Look, one night I was at a card game with a mess of performers, and Cary, all of us, we were saying: what if we all had somewhere to go up, somewhere out of the city, somewhere up in the mountains, somewhere to rest outta the lights?"

"Don't rich people have places like that already?"

"Sure, but it's never organized. You gotta do it all on your lonesome."

"What's wrong with that?"

"What's wrong with that? What's wrong with that, she asks!" He tapped his fists on the dashboard gamely. "You get to be famous and you get used to the idea you don't have to think of the details. So I asked Marjorie to make us sandwiches and we sat up all night, devising a kind of, what, spread, not a home for retired actors, but, see, a kind of lodge." We drove past the prehistoric silhouettes of backhoes and trenchers, the mud fields shadowed and tread combed.

"You thought of the details."

"Yes, but you see, it was a game."

I made a minor sound so he'd continue. I wanted to consume only. Perhaps it was like a dream, having him beside me: a man full of symbols I did not want to decode. A man I wanted to witness in a solemn or laughing fashion.

"The sun came up and everyone begged off but I had the month away from set, so I got to thinking. Somewhere for resting and hunting and cooking like I liked to do. Not that you'd know about any of that."

"I'm not a very good hobbyist."

"Don't beat yourself up. A lady has much to occupy her time."

"So what did you do? Did you buy a place?"

"Buy a place? Sister, I built it."

"Did you go up there away from the lights?"

"I did."

"And did anyone else?"

"They visited me a time or two, to make use of my fine hunting dogs who I liked to spoil. They were mutts mostly, for anyone knew they were better creatures than the purebreds: black and tans crossed with blue ticks, redbone-black labs, a bit o' terrier in that handsome retriever."

I sighed loudly to stop him but he kept on.

"Only Lucie was purebred, but even so she was a whippety lil' gal, the runtiest of runts, forty pounds soaking, a hard mouth wouldn't let go of anything till I asked her the umpteenth time. Don't tell Marjorie lest she get jealous: once I had my haven, I let all the pups up on the bed with me. Course that was my comfort much as theirs: *three dog night* ain't come from nothing. Boy, with them in the bed I'd wake up sweating in the dead of winter!"

We were moving closer to my place. Here the buildings were fully built, dense and orderly, a series of shapes repeated. No one was about. The car's hum burgeoned against the edges of my neighbors' cars and siding and mailboxes. I tried to remember what movie or book had taught me about hunting dogs. I wondered about all the things I had learned and forgotten, in the encroaching, milky mist of trying to be okay.

"But mostly you were up there by yourself? Didn't you have movies to shoot?"

"Oh, that was after my career."

I thought of the genial retirement Pop would never have: a sunny golf green where he played half-heartedly, boating with Ma on the Bay, looking up childhood friends on the internet— no, this was merely a brochure of retirement. I thought instead—

"I got sick and had to leave the place."

I didn't say anything. I wanted to change the channel.

"Yes, a man has got to find a place or patch of land for himself," Gene said.

"What about the ladies?" I asked, turning and scanning the empty road. This felt in some way exhilarating. I was unemployed, moving swiftly from harmless kook to edge-dweller. I was ready to end this day. I was ready to discover how next I would degrade.

"Ladies we love live on in our hearts," he said. "And that's all there is to it."

"You've never much gone in for ladies, have you?" I said.

"Yes, well, now, I mean, what I'd have all those wives for? But no, you're right. Never got the hang of them."

"I got the hang of you," I said.

"And ain't it just grand!"

Nothing was grand. I parked in front of my quiet vinyl-sided eight-flat and nodded at him. "Home we go?" As we walked down the little path to the apartment door, we linked our arms.

At the door Geney kissed me on the forehead. He smelled of nothing, but also of bitter bay cologne and an herbal after-shave. "Good night, little one," he said. "A bit of sleep is all you need." This wasn't true.

I bowed adieu and went inside. The air inside was cold and shocking, as it had been at my parents' home. In this family we controlled our interior climates with severity. I sat on the love-seat, between the kitchenette and bed, and breathed out loud enough for the neighbors to hear. I wondered if they were disturbed by the noise: I used to worry that I thought about all of the wrong things while the right things went slipping by.

THE NEXT MORNING I woke accordioned in the loveseat. On my phone there were two voicemails: one morning call from Ma, and one from Ken. Ken had texted also, to say that he loved me, was thinking of me, would call later. I thought I should lose his number. Instead I responded aloud to myself that I, too, felt love; then got a glass of water and folded myself into the loveseat again and began to braid my hair into tiny trellises. It was something Ma had done for me when I was a kid, out of the bath and just before bed. Over breakfast I'd undo the braids, my hair falling into loose crimps. Throughout the day the texture would relax until my hair was straight again. Now I had no hair ties. The braids undid themselves as quickly as I finished them. Yet I continued the ritual. I thought of Gene's retirement home for actors, at its full capacity: one man, several dogs, and a whole lotta bluster.

In my eyes and chest I felt, still, the logy, sentimental press of a lingering hangover. I didn't know how Ma felt, nor Pop. Ken, by habit and goodwill, had adhered to our family despite his evident normalcy; he knew how to feel and express like a real person. So I knew that the night prior—as I'd sighed and prattled to no one—he'd been home lying on his tidy bed watching the ceiling for some extraordinary permission to cry. Probably it was one of his life's central pits that he ended up in our strange herd. He was always so healthy and tall. A kind, soft stomach. Dark hair, a broken eyetooth.

Sometime after college, I'd asked him why he didn't get it fixed.

"I don't know," he'd said.

"It's probably expensive," I'd said. "Who has the money?"

"Does it give me character?" He'd presented his choppers.

"No," I'd said. "But it makes me wanna buy you dinner."

Briefly I wondered if I should call Ken; I didn't want to. It didn't occur to me he might like or need some comfort or company.

When my hands grew tired of braiding I realized that I needed something heftier to occupy myself. The notion of anything readily available—TV, text, tunes—made me dizzy. I decided I'd go into the city and look at something or somethings, pretend to be in and of the world. Through the glass of the back door I could see a squirrel picking its way through the brush of the shared lawn.

My phone was vibrating on the floor beside me, this time a call from a number I didn't recognize. I rose to stretch and dress. I checked the listings for current exhibits. I made provisional choices regarding my day. When ready I listened to the voicemail the caller had left.

Monica. Had I given her my number? It seemed so. "Look," she said. "It's no good you haven't been anywhere I have." It had only been two days since I'd met her. I put the phone on speaker and let her voice fill the room. It had been a long time since I'd had a new friend. She said, "Call." She said, "Soon." I wanted to know why she'd really called, but on the other hand I thought I might not care.

I didn't listen to the remaining voicemails, instead departing quickly and driving through summer-light traffic to the Metro station's Park & Ride. I intended to visit the Portrait Gallery: to stare at the faces of old white men, to have some staring contests, to always lose or always win. It would give me a clean minute. A breath in which not to think. I liked being inside museum buildings. I was less invested, still, in the art.

At the station I scanned my card and took the escalator up to the platform. It looked like rain. I sniffed the hot asphalt flux of the city. The train came quickly.

Boarding I saw the car was packed. There must've been, I believe, some kind of event that had attracted tourists to the Red Line in August. Most locals—if they had any money, vacation time, or otherwise-sourced mobility—knew to leave the city's boggy haze. Or they stayed inside, orienting sticky skin toward any source of cool. Meanwhile the interlopers emerged, coming by threes and fours and fives and twenties, on buses and airplanes, to see the nation's capital, and to sweat.

In this sea of raucous motley tourists in baseball caps and pleated shorts, my body ached. I searched for a place to rest. A rich- and young-looking businessman was taking up two-and-a-half seats with a rolling suitcase and garment bag. It was the solo sitting prospect. I perched beside the suitcase. "Is this your bag?" I asked him. The train began to move and in response he moved his bag only slightly. It made no spatial difference. I watched him chuckle to himself while my leg muscles propped me, bleating. On his phone he was reading from a satirical news-humor site. I scanned his hands. He did not wear a ring but rather a bracelet of Tibetan prayer beads. Paired with the suit and behavior I found this accessory an odious display of hope. The man put his phone away, then yawned and smiled to himself. My calf muscles seized as the train skittered along. His glasses were rimless, his shirt primly pressed.

"Excuse me," I said. "Do you think you could move your bags a bit more?" He looked at me as if smelling something. Other passengers leaned in to see what he would do. He did not move. He took out his phone and began to read the satirical news again, overplaying his chuckle.

To match I sighed like a brat. "Excuse me. Maybe you also need space and care," I said to him. "Maybe you are also on your way to a funeral." I was not dressed for a funeral, was wearing shabby jeans and some T-shirt with the sleeves cut off. Like a man I gambled my umbrage would get me what I wanted. This time he looked up at me.

Gene was sardine-packed upright on a pole two thirds of the way down the car. Even so, I could see him clenching his ham fists white. At this point everyone was paying attention but no one was doing anything. I had been loud over the tourist chatter. It began to rain, hot lashes of water whipping the train windows, tightening the scene.

The man said something that sounded like "I do not speak English." Though he had just been reading it. I could not tell if he cared that he was a known liar. Geney was boiling. All around the tourists made satisfied humming noises. No one knew he was a liar but me. A girl my own age offered me her seat. I said no thanks. I watched the graffiti on the buildings go by, wet colors overlapping with speed. I burned a bit. I fantasized about a retirement home for twenty-something women with antisocial tendencies. Presently I felt squashed.

When at last we rolled into the station I deboarded in an extravagant, silent huff. A busker violinist was playing "Flight of the Bumblebee." I recognized it from *The Jack Benny Program*, which Pop loved to listen to on Sunday nights, courtesy *The Big Broadcast* with Ed Walker. Pop loved everything old. Once, he'd liked to hold on; now he was letting it all ride. I moved out and down G Street through a blood-warm rain, up the Gallery's broad steps, and in.

The Portrait Gallery was not as popular as, say, the Air and Space—where once they'd had a Star Trek exhibition, and where they sold the tantalizing tooth/tongue challenge of astronaut ice cream in the extensive gift shop. Here, the galleries were inflected occasionally by bored-looking, backpack-wearing groups of two or three, who spent twenty-to-forty seconds standing near each painting. Their patterned duty of tourism put me off. Despite my previous plan I bypassed the dry-rot presidential faces. At *Mr. Hackett, in the Character of Rip Van Winkle* I stopped, simply because there was no one else nearby. My rain-wet skin frosted in the gallery's cool.

In *Van Winkle*, a young actor performs as an old man who has not experienced his own life. This man stands beseeching, in a lovely primeval forest, with one arm stretched toward the heavens and the other at his chest. The painting is made in the moment of Rip's waking. He wears a tattered shift and breeches, coma wrinkled. His features are childlike, eyes doll round, with a nimbus-y beard, bald pate, and long white hair. It is supposed to be a maybe-comic picture, or maybe a comic role wrought as a tragic picture, or maybe the other way around. The curatorial notes relayed: Rip Van Winkle went up a mountain with his dog and rifle, lay down to nap and slept for decades, woke to find his beard long and his wife dead and his son a man.

It's a story about time, and its passing. Of having no familiarity with a place that was once home. The idea of legacy is, in the end, impossible. Okay: I knew the painting was there. I think I wanted to feel accused, flung. I wanted to press on a personal bruise.

"I woulda made a great Van Winkle!" Geney whispered. I rolled my eyes. "A non-actor cannot understand how it feels to encounter yourself in a role!" His whisper tickled my lobes. I went out of the museum.

Outside the summer shower had ended. As I walked down 9th, water steamed from the grass. The stone buildings lightened as they dried. Gene trotted alongside me, making no noise on the wet gravel as we crossed the Mall. "A man out of time!" he persisted. "Who better to play him than yours truly?"

"It's almost like a bee is buzzing in my ear," I said.

I bought a Chipwich from a kiosk beside the carousel and sat on a bench, watching as kids throttled the necks of the carousel horses and screamed in delight and terror equally.

I thought of returning Ken's call, but he was at work until later. Also I didn't feel like I wanted to hear anything he'd say. "Gene?" I asked the humid air.

"Denise?" he answered, rematerializing, looking tired. "Did I ever tell you about the time?"

"About what time?" I allowed my eyes to unfocus, so I didn't have to see the throttling children.

"About the time I up and left everybody?" I shook my head, though he had. He was a record skipping. I had no verve to move the needle, to get up and lift the arm. "I'll tell you I was troubled by the Soviet attitude toward the German State from the start. It was pushy—that's an understatement. They had nukes or almost did. They couldn't be bossed or reasoned with."

"Who does that sound like to you?" I asked, a bit bored.

"It wasn't safe."

"What wasn't?"

"Anywhere where there were a lot of people, anywhere they could do a lot of harm."

I thought then of the packed train car and the lazy and/or territorial man. How he must have been desperate in a crowd to build private space. I only blamed him a little. I thought how I was becoming less invested in what a body could or couldn't make happen. I was simply a defenseless meatbag. A stroller came by and spit a spray of gravel at my ankles. "Here's to mud in your eye!" I said or thought.

"You said it." Gene continued: "So that's when I decided to buy a large parcel of land outside Imnaha, Oregon, where the river and Big Sheep Creek come together. I began to stay at the spread for a week, then go back into town, do some flight runs, get paid, and then get back there, safe and sound." I wanted to ask him was he an actor or a pilot. A ghost or a man.

When Gene and I first met I'd been in the bath, wondering whether Ma would let me go on the Colonial Williamsburg field trip. I had been newly fifteen, inventorying my own body. I saw it was hard but softening, follicles spitting. I sank, letting the water enter my ear holes.

From under the water I'd heard a snuffly basso.

When I came back up, well, there was Gene, sitting on top of the closed toilet, humming a nothing tune in that voice made of simple syrup and rocks. I almost asked him to pass the conditioner, was how little strange it occurred to me then. After all, my father was dying and my body was changing and I was thinking I did not know or understand what permanence was supposed to mean. So I said: "Hello?"

"Listen kid I gotta tongue twister for ya," he debuted. I was dumb; he rapped on the tub. "Hello? Hello? I have a tongue twister. You interested?"

"Fuck off," I said. I had never said this to anyone. He made a *huh* of a laugh and seemed otherwise untroubled. Bathwater rolled from my scalp down the sides of my head, setting my shoulders to shiver. I saw he was wearing a broad tweed coat and pantaloons. I made my chest concave, dipping my chin back into the water.

"Do you want to hear my tongue twister?" he asked again.

"Sure, yeah," I said. I worked my mouth open and closed to distract myself from my embarrassment. Each time my jaw moved it made a little eddy. "Lay it on me."

"Okay, okay, okay, okay, here ya go." He put his hands up as if pushing against a pane of glass. "You ready?"

I nodded.

"Who eats floating fish but flies?"

"I don't get it," I said, sitting up and splashing the surface with one forefinger. I discovered that his presence did not make me feel shy. Mostly this was because he was a figment. Also: bodies are bodies. Everyone's got one, till they don't. "What do you mean?"

"Girlie, there's nothing to get. Who eats floating fish but flies? Say it five times fast."

"Who eats floating flish but flies," I said, on the first try-out.

He laughed at me. "See? I told ya. Wait for a bona fide performer to try it out." He made a little show of clearing his throat and then began: "Who eats floating fish but flies. Who eats floating fish but flies. Who eats floating fish but flies. Who eats floating fish but flies. Who eats floating fish but flies." He said it like he was walking across a tightrope that was also a country lane. "Stick with me, kid, and you'll see."

I sank my head back under the water and blew bubbles, up. The bath was warm as urine. Underneath it was all slangy shadow and rippling light. Surfacing I thought maybe I should ask him to further elaborate, but he was already gone. But I needn't have worried or wondered. He'd come back, again and again.

Now on the Mall Gene was still prattling about his fortress-cum-Shangri-La. "I had lettuces and beefsteak tomatoes, snap beans and a little row of corn at the edge of the land where the cattle couldn't get at it."

"I will at some point," I interrupted, "want to know what this has got to do with me." I felt irritable all over again. This feeling was a generic distraction.

"O but what hasn't it got to do with you!" Gene cracked his meaty, sweaty knuckles and seesawed on the bench. "Every story has a lesson! Every riddle has an answer! Every joke can get a laugh!"

I said that I had never been good at punchlines.

"You're wasting my time, if that's what you think," he said. I agreed. I recalled then Hill's finger pet. I recalled my body, touched, and shuddered in this until diverted by a runny mush in my hands. It was the Chipwich, which I had neglected unto its melting. I threw it out and washed my hands in a water fountain whose drain was clotted with snot.

My head felt full and sloshing. I decided to ford the crowds, and descended into the subterranean. There the station was mostly empty; a suited man on the opposite platform also waited. I thought: Is that the man who would not cede his seat for me, a declared funeral-goer in need of space and care? He was standing, erect and free of his bags, twenty feet across and five feet over, beyond my track and the next. It was or was not him. We stood in the barrel-vaulted concrete volume, our bodies minor beneath its curve. As I opened my mouth I understood I was heading in a new direction and had been for some time. I submitted to this and hollered across the tracks.

"Where are your prayer beads?"

"What?" he hollered back.

"Where—is—your—bracelet?" The question echoed dully in the big space.

He looked confused and it was not quickly or slowly but instantly that I acknowledged to myself that this was a different man. He was similar only in stature and posture, in whiteness and maleness. I wished for either train to arrive, to carry one of us out of this scene. One did not for quite some time.

Meanwhile we pretended that I hadn't said anything. More people congregated around us. The train came. I got on it. I was hungry, and wished I'd remembered to eat my ice cream. This time I found a seat, and soon closed my eyes all the way to my stop.

On through the station, onto the parking garage, and there to my hot car, in which I sat, blank. Still I did not want to talk to anyone I knew. I had no job. My father was finally dying; my mother was fixated. I longed for crowds or to become anonymous, even to myself. Why not, in this condition, meet a stranger for a coffee date?

Monica answered quickly. She named a location near the research campus, a day—the next so-called work day, a Monday—and a time—lunch o'clock. All the rest of the day and night I did nothing but sleep, waking occasionally to look at the squirrel out on the back grass, which was either the squirrel from the morning or a different one, or perhaps it wasn't there at all.

"MARK SAID YOU had a nice body," Monica said. "At least you eat croissants." We were in a chain cafe in a strip mall. Monica saluted my pastry. To this I grunted low. She gave me a funny look. The confidential dearness of the other night was entirely gone and in its place, this—this womanly collegial air. There was a summer afternoon melee of readers and klatschers and sticky young families, two messy ginger-headed children sitting under a corner table, their mother fussing with her phone. It wasn't the kind of place I liked to be.

"Oh," I said finally, realizing she was expecting an answer. "I like them. So I do."

"That's perfectly logical, I guess, but anyway." She swallowed a bit of coffee. "Anyway. Mark would like to see you again, I think. He hasn't said anything directly, but I can tell. I saw him yesterday night. He usually doesn't bother to mention girls, you know, after the fact."

"I'm not looking for anything, I think."

"Oh, well." Her blunt bangs reorganized themselves as she

wrinkled her brow. "Well. We liked you." And after a moment: "It's nice anyway, then," she said, "to be spending time with another woman of science for once."

"It's not that I don't want female friends," I said carefully. "It's just that I don't have them."

"Well, in science—" she swallowed, "whatever you do, there still aren't an embarrassment of ladies."

"An embarrassment of ladies," I repeated.

"Yes. It isn't a nail salon, for god sakes." Monica seemed to notice I wasn't saying anything of my own. I wondered if she cared what I thought of her. "It can just be a bit of, well, a boys' club." Is it possible to be both warm and awful? Witness this specimen, doing the best she can.

"I guess," I responded. "I haven't really noticed." I felt she was probably wrong, that there were many female scientists, not a majority, but definitely, like, a squadron's worth, and that perhaps the ones she knew were simply too challenging or mouthy for her taste. There had been plenty in my own former lab, not that I had spoken to any of them. Now all these years later I imagine it's different—better, even, perhaps. Not that time and progress are always companions.

"Perhaps you wouldn't," she said.

"It seems to be an even split around where I work, especially with all the young kids, in from school."

"Yes, but well, that happens later." She swept her hand upward and back in a wave-like motion. "I saw a lot of female colleagues go into, I don't know, social work, administration, their degrees just sitting there. Or just having those." She tipped her head toward the mother with the ginger kids, the little one cleaned up now and the older one set upon the frosting part of a cupcake.

"Oh," I said once more, and filled my mouth with air.

"Well, you just—in the sciences you have to want it. In anything really."

"Yes," I said. "I see," I said. Even strangers were overrated.

"Lots of people can be better than you—smarter, better looking, more inventive," Monica said. "But you can still want something the most, and that can be your edge. Well—" she said, angling her head like an overselling actor. "What's your edge?"

"I don't really know."

"You've got to have one."

"I'm not sure I do."

"I can tell you do, though."

"I feel edgeless," I said. My honesty shocked me. But I went on. "Or right now I do. I have some family things going on, and I've just left my job." I could not stop from saying it. Likely it was my fatigue and the strange man on the train and all the sleeping and possibly the croissant. Already I was imagining that its butter was getting handsy with my insides, laminating me. "Something to do with hours and funding not going through and some line on the budget," I added. My body calmed.

"I hadn't realized." She looked caught. I thought maybe she wasn't so happy to find herself having coffee with an unemployed person.

"My last day was the one I met you all," I continued.

"Well that explains it!" She smiled.

"Explains what?"

"Oh, how sloshed you got." I felt the hot red of a blush start at my jaw. She pretended not to see. "What do you think you'll do next?"

"Next?" It was a reasonable question I supposed. Just not one I had thought of.

"For a job or whatever."

"I thought I'd take some time—" I started.

"Oh totally!" she interrupted. "I took some time before my postdoc. Went to Cyprus and ate a lot of fish and drank grappa with the locals. Or it wasn't called grappa, but it basically was grappa, something with a *z*, anyway. I didn't know a soul there." With a prideful commercial smile she gulped some coffee and kept going. I affected a pose of care by tipping my head to one side. "I think it was really brave of me to, you know, just go there. My mother was so worried. But it was just fine. Really very freeing."

"I'm not sure that's exactly my style—"

"Well you don't have to go to Cyprus. There's loads of places to go. Someplace with more Americans, maybe? Saint Martin or Jamaica, or maybe a cruise? They have all those cruises now for young people, not just moldy retirees."

"I do have a nut socked away," I said, slowly cottoning. It was true that there was only so much money that Ma would allow me to contribute to the family fund, only so much that I spent on beer and wine while hanging out with Ken. Rent was not so much. My debt, too, was wan: A confluence of in-state tuition, income-based repayment plans, and lucky employment had made me in this way exceptional. In my account there was a modest overage: fiscal responsibility by chance and luck. I was not planning for the future, anyway.

"Smart girl," Monica said. "If you wanted something more low-maintenance, you could go hiking, the Appalachian Trail, or, that's a bit dramatic, maybe just part of it? I had friends in school who did that on summer break, they came back all fit and tan with the funniest trail names . . ." When I didn't say anything for a beat, she continued. "It's a thing, now, isn't it?" she said or asked. "For a young woman such as yourself or even myself to go on a great adventure?" She grinned and the perfection of her teeth seemed to me horrible.

"I'll have to see," I said. "It may be hard to get away right now, but it's possible, I guess." The idea hung there in the air and neither of us spoke.

Monica stroked one side of her hair with both hands at once, a sort of vain but absentminded gesture. "Well," she said finally. "I think I recommend it. At the very least, if you really won't see Mark again, that's your business, but you have to promise to be my friend."

I realized two things: that I did not believe her, and that I felt that she had some ulterior motive. I was not interested in uncovering it. There was nothing from Monica I wanted. For example: in her presence, I was pretending to be digestible. This fatiguing act wasn't worth an encore.

I pictured myself raising up and away from the table. In the corner, the mother with the phone was trying to feed her ginger toddler, while her girl ran through the aisles brandishing a plastic wand. At once the toddler spit up on himself, all down the front of his shirt, and the little girl tripped over somebody's laptop case and began to cry miserably. Everyone looked up for a moment at the noise, like some herd of hunted animals, and then, evaluating the situation as nonthreatening, dipped their heads back down to attend to their sandwiches and pastries and spreadsheets and books and beverages.

Monica's phone chirped from her purse and she withdrew it, glancing at the screen. "I'm afraid I've got to jet," she said, balling her napkin and dropping it into her half-full cup. I watched the paper succumb to the liquid; to amuse myself I winked at it. "I told Omar I'd pick him up from the mechanic in Bethesda. His Saab is on the fritz."

"Okay," I said, summoning some bright smile.

"I'll be working on a deadline all next week," she said, rising. "But the first weekend of every month I get together with a bunch of other women—don't worry, it's not all hen-clucking, if that's what you're thinking—it'd just be nice to have some new blood in the group, especially since I already know I like you." She stood over me. "You're an original, Denise."

I had no idea what she meant, except that I was different from her.

"It's a date," I said, and she stooped to kiss me on the cheek and said goodbye, moving smoothly and elegantly away. I wouldn't go to the women's group, I already knew. But she was right about something: I needed an out. Even my imaginary friend had said so. I'm not thick: I understood that his obsession regarding escape was my own.

Though later in the car I found I couldn't imagine where I

would go, nor for how long, nor how I would explain it to frantic Ma, or dying Pop. An image popped up in my mind, and it was ole Van Winkle, unbidden, his confused young-old face beseeching questioningly into upper air. I imagined I would stay. I did not yet understand that courage was unrequired in making such a decision. Only a dynamic cycle of folly, and an inability to break same.

Once home, I took a shower and washed the plate and cup in the sink. This was a game of delay. For soon I found myself back on the loveseat, searching internet listings on my laptop for house rentals at random. It was that day, or maybe the day after, or even one week later, that I found the listing. For a while I held the secret of my plan in a determined, dusty part of my mind. GET AWAY the listing headline read:

> Old cabin, running well water, no electricity, working wood stove, outhouse. Perfect for a quiet stay. Must travel by air or hike several days. This is not a convenient location. I have spent a lot of time talking to people who don't realize there is not a grocery store down the block or cell phone reception. So I would appreciate it if you thought first before contacting me.

Feeling like I was on a kind of drug, I dashed off an email, said I was an artist. Needed solitude, etc. Collaborators would come in spring. Federal grant. Good wilderness experience.

Basic water safety training. Was there water nearby? How could I get there, and how soon?

Meet me at the outfitter, the guy wrote back the next morning. Here's the address. Here's my number. For an additional fee, I'll fly you up soon as you want. He attached pictures of the cabin but I didn't open the files; they seemed like a trick for which I didn't want to fall. I didn't know if or when I would go, but having those unopened files was almost enough. To see a door did not mean you had to go through it. The man said I could take my time. That the calendar was open and he'd let me know if anything changed. I sent him a deposit and wondered whether I'd follow. In the meantime I memorized the digits of his telephone number, repeating them in an incantation, an inexact effort to self-soothe.

THE REST OF August drained out with a slurp. Pop worsened, a boat straining toward the horizon line as Ma tethered him ever closer. I couldn't stand to be with them. I hardly spoke to Ken, who forgave me daily, while I thought less of him for it.

Each day I thought of the remote cabin. The thought of it condensed in me until I was unable to ignore it. I'm sure I did things, fed myself, and slept, commiserated with my loved ones in a foot-out-the-door sort of way, told Gene not to bother me. I did not look for a job. Instead I read discussion forums on the internet about how to live in the woods, sewed over the seams of clothing and bags so they wouldn't rip under stress of use. I went to used bookstores and bought outdated wilderness guides for a dollar apiece. In a dresser drawer I located my knife. Its

handle was shaped like a hummingbird, with a rainbow tita-
nium finish.

Compulsively I gathered supplies: dry foods, several cases of
meal replacement bars in "berry blast" and "mocha buzz" flavors, outerwear and thermals, a tarp, some flares, a compass, a
case of applicator-free tampons, a good carbon steel knife, plastic tubs to put it all in. I made an inventory list, and found an
ad for a truck and traded in my sedan. I put the list in the glove
box and felt pricked. Gene laughed at me, holding his belly.
"Whaddya think you're doing?" he asked. I ignored him and he
took it personally like I wanted him to.

When Ma asked why I'd traded in the sedan, I reminded
her how I'd always wanted a pickup. I never had. There were no
follow-ups: to help with the medical bills Ma had taken a part-
time job in the administrative pool at the county offices. She had
no time to afford me extra scrutiny. Pop declined, and quickly. I
blossomed into a private nut. My escape plan thrummed in my
chest.

I began to divest myself of any unuseful possessions. I got rid
of it all quietly, surely; the box of personal stuff, I burned one
night on a picnic area grill in the park down the street. The filial
bric-a-brac I secretly dropped into decorative boxes at the family
home: some 3x5s, a bracelet, a medal. While doing so I purloined
a vial of Pop's pain pills, just in case. Lest you think me cruel, he
had many other such vials, and refills to spare. Internet aided, I
sold most everything else, called Purple Heart to pick up the rest.
Not once did I think about how it would be, once I was there.

When it was September I gave my landlord a month of

notice. She shrugged, or whatever the vocal version of that is, on the phone over a shitty connection from Delaware where she was taking care of her own sick father, who had dementia. Everywhere in my periphery parents expired or were expiring. Meanwhile I found my skin sensitive, my feelings changeable. I woke up with a rosy rash across my sternum. I burped meals I couldn't remember chewing. Any noise made my heart flop, scare, shimmer.

Meanwhile I attempted to look like I was staying put. I said yes to things I would've rather said no to, just to keep this up:

I watched, one day, as inside the old Hecht's department store Ma riffled the bedding displays in a manner more intense than I would've liked. "It's a gloomy kind of blue, yeah?" Ma asked, holding a pillow in front of her face. We stood at a display by the escalators.

I had to admit that it was gloomy. "Gray undertones."

"Yes, gray. Gray green. Very 'painting of a stormy sea.'"

"But not just a stormy sea?"

"No, a bad painting of one. Just slightly more yellow than the real thing." I had not known she was so sensitive about color. Or maybe she had not before been. Pop was trying out a newly hired nurse. We were trying out a newly hired nurse. Figuring out if we could tolerate a stranger. I could. But I was leaving. She'd asked me to accompany her on this errand. I had consented, knowing how soon I hoped to betray or relieve her with my departure.

We had decided to go to the bad mall instead of the rich mall, because there was better parking and fewer aggressive consumers with nowhere else to put their anger and dissatisfaction regarding the vagaries of contemporary life as humans residing in the suburbs, U.S.A. In the county's northwesterly portion, closer to the lab, we could have expected a wide selection of upper-tier chain restaurants, sports utility vehicle dodging, a constant parabolic titter of teens wielding credit cards the balances of which they would never see. In the early days of the first cancer, Ken and I had gone there occasionally, to bum cigarettes from the uncaring adults dragging by the seasonal topiaries, then roll through the interior luxury, our brains buzzing slightly.

In the one-level-plus-basement mall Ma and I had chosen, there were a few manicure places, an eyeglass store, a place to buy midrange wedding bands, an "urban footwear" boutique, a Sears that always had appliances on special. There were often stores in the process of closing (a camera shop, a by-the-pound candy store with twenty-four flavors of jelly beans—each flavor's contents having massed together by age, heat, and dust) or opening (a teen clothing place that seemed to specialize in man-made fabrics, an international imports boutique). This mall often had a serene, ghost town feeling. It was somewhere we could feel inconspicuous and/or at home.

Near the bedding display there were two sales associates chatting, taking turns holding up blouses for each other's appraisal. A bent-over elderly man was working his way at a traffic jam pace from the outer entrance toward the central floor. I picked up another blue bolster pillow and tossed it into the air. There its center of gravity stuttered. I fumbled it on the way down and it landed beneath the stand-mixers. When I came back from retrieving it, Ma was still hugging her own pillow, looking somewhere in the direction of the shoe department. "Ma?" I asked. "Earth to Ma."

"Ma to Earth," she replied without looking at me, and put the pillow down.

We were fetching the perfume she liked. When she and Pop had first been married, he had often surprised her with small gifts. This perfume had been one of the most common selections. It smelled of musk and amber and orange blossom, and came in a faceted diamond-shaped bottle, its bottom blunted such that it could sit flat. Now I imagine it on dressers and bathroom counters and nightstands across the universe. An intimate thing, duplicated so many times.

"What do you need? Do you need anything?" Ma asked, as we moved to the cosmetic area. "Do you need a scent? Do you need a pair of boots before winter?"

"A scent?" Everything around us was beige or chrome or gold or glass. The floors were dirty but the lights were bright. "No, Ma, I don't need anything, I told you." I pictured Pop asleep. I pictured the stranger watching him. I tried to tell if I could worry about it. I wondered what was Ma thinking. "I don't need anything," I repeated.

"Okay, okay." She sauntered through the environs of commerce, as if she were any woman. I allowed myself to feel briefly ambivalent, then remembered: GET AWAY. The clarion call of the oversaturated and truly cracked. All over again I lit up and thrilled.

We floated to the appropriate counter. The woman behind it wore a flatteringly cut lab coat and a full face of makeup. Her lab coat hardly cued a thought about the one I'd previously worn. My thrill regarding the future was munching my near-past. I wondered what the saleswoman's face would look like in sunlight, with all that lacquer. I never wore makeup and imagined those who did were hiding, not accentuating.

The woman in the lab coat led my mother to the fragrance area as the employees giggled, plucking and replacing blouses in plaids and dots and stripes. I wondered what it would be like to live in the woods. My phone vibrated. It was a text from Ken, wondering if we were even friends anymore. Would I reply; I replaced my phone in my pocket.

"This one has notes of lavender, which is very calming."

"It always makes me sneeze."

"Okay, yes, that's common. What about this one? It's earthy, very seasonal."

"A little too much for me, I think. I like a delicate smell."

"This one's based in rose. Very feminine."

"A little too young, maybe."

"It reminds me of walking through the garden."

"A lovely notion."

"Yes."

"I think I'll just take this one, the two ounce, the eau de toilette. Just a little treat."

"Nice," the woman in the lab coat said. "Nice." She didn't seem to mean it.

There was no more speaking and I looked up to see Ma and

the woman both agog in the same direction. It was a slow fist of seconds as they began to take action, moving from the counter. Only then did I think to look in that direction also, where the old man was now stomach-down on the walkway. His body wrenched and twitched; I wondered why I hadn't heard the fall.

Ma and the woman and the nearby employees all entered the frame jogging. One or another flipped the old man over. The perfume woman cradled his head, snatched a blouse from a nearby rack and stuffed its polyblend into his mouth, told someone to call the EMTs. My mother held his legs; it was a kind and exciting position; I stood ten feet away. I was shaking.

"Come get his arms!" the perfume woman called. They were swinging from his sides like combines. I sauntered to his spasming body. From closer up I could see his eyes rolling back into his head, his face flushed. He smelled of talc and rot and this filled my nostrils as I tried to hold his wrists at his sides.

An EMT showed up and asked us all to stand back. She removed the blouse and rolled the man to his side. "Don't ever put anything in a seizing man's mouth!" she yelled. "And don't restrain him!" She was my age and seemed genuinely angry at us, had on strict navy garb. From the margins we watched the old man's spit come in threads from his mouth. It made a small puddle on the smudgy linoleum.

"Do you think we can go?" Ma asked into my ear, right beside me.

"Do you think we should stay?"

"What can we do? We helped when we could." Then Ma began to walk back to the outer entrance.

"That was weird," I said, once we had exited the store into a heavy heat that set upon our edges.

She said: "I'm sorry not to have gotten the perfume." I told her I'd pick it up on the way from work one of these days. I wouldn't. "Better go to the other mall," Ma said, not really looking at anything. As if wealth guarded from infirmity. I wondered what her finances were like. It occurred to me that I should know something like that.

IT WAS ONLY later, while stopped at a red light, that I saw Ma was crying quietly. "Oh, Ma," I said.

"It's okay," she said. "I'm okay." She seemed aggravated I was paying her mind. Or was I imagining this, hoping?

The whole way back to the house I asked inconsequential questions. "Do you want the radio on?" "Are you too cold?" "AC down?" "Windows down?" "Want to take my sunglasses?" I drove cleanly along familiar suburban routes. There was the bank, the bank, the post office, the fire station, the fruit stand. The carpet store, the church, the church, the temple. The office plaza, the apartment buildings, the fast food joints. "Want me to come hang out?" I asked, when I pulled into the driveway. "I just have a few errands to run later."

Ma's eyes were no longer watery. Her face was a windless thing. We said goodbye.

"How did Pop like the nurse?" I asked the next day, via phone. Ma said he liked her fine.

•

IN EARLY SEPTEMBER Ken went away to visit his mom and sister in Fayetteville, where they'd moved after we'd finished high school. Now I didn't have to lay out so much time dodging his calls. It'd be easier, I felt, if I left before Ken returned. Meanwhile Pop got worse. Ma called to tell me she'd hired the nurse for good. The woman gave her a deal, she reported— "I think she pities me." I told her people in that line of work don't traffic in pity like that. She asked, "When did I become someone to pity?"

Since always, I thought. This sounded cruel even to me. I had everything packed in the truck bed, under a cap. My apartment was empty, move-in ready. I said bye to Ma and began to pace the place studiously, as if in the market for a rental. "What are the utility bills like, per month?" I asked an imaginary agent. "Is there any history of flooding?" I ran my hands along the clean old laminate of the kitchen counter. I turned the bathroom faucets on and off. "Good water pressure. That can be hard to find." I scanned the tub, saw the chips in the tile floor. "Do they allow pets? I was thinking of getting something small."

In the living area Gene was waiting for me. "They don't allow dogs or cats, but you could have a fish or turtle or even a guinea pig, I'm sure. Something that doesn't need to leave its cage much," he said. He was wearing a creased gray suit and looked almost handsome. One corner of his lapel bent the wrong way. I surveyed the marks I'd made on the floor and walls while removing my possessions. Empty, the place looked bald. "But a fish," he continued, "is hardly trusty as a dog."

"I don't know."

"I know this is at the top of your budget," he said. "But you won't find better value."

"Oh, I think it's fine. Just not for me."

"Do you have an idea of what is for you?" He crossed the room and stood professional. "I do have other properties."

"More outdoor space," I said. "Wood floors."

"People always say they like wood floors and I don't understand it!"

I said I thought they were nice.

"Well they're hard to keep clean. Your guests are always tracking in mud and dust, and what are you going to do: sweep all hours of the day?" I coughed; he went on: "No, give me something fine as wall-to-wall! A luxurious pile. A classy color. Heck, what's more important in an apartment than soundproofing?"

"You may be right, but just the same I'll keep looking," I said. We were playing some kind of game, pretending we were not who we were.

He walked to the door and opened it for me. I kept waiting for him to acknowledge who we really were. "You women," he spat. "You don't know what's best!"

I stood in the doorway steaming. "Who does!"

"You ladies need someone to guide you—someone who sees the bigger picture."

"Someone like you?" I stepped closer to him. "Would you like to teach a lady what she needs?" I brushed the dented shoulder pad of his jacket. I breathed.

"I've got a wife, lady. Her name is Marjorie and she likes the finer things—"

"Wouldn't Marjorie want to know that you're working so hard to make money so she can have those finer things?" I curled around him: a snake, a rope, a scarf. The door was still open. Who knows what I looked like.

"Miss, I must stop this," Gene protested. He moved his big body away from me and down the front walk.

"Fine," I called. "But I don't want you coming back here, begging." And then I laughed!

He dematerialized. I shut the door. I was once more myself only, exhausted all over again. I began to understand: My plan was not only an escape but a removal. Better to save my loved ones from this monster I was, a person who'd run off her own imaginary friend, addled by everything in sight.

SOON IT WAS the second week of September. Straightaway, I fixed to leave, but things kept snapping me off my trail.

Once, construction jammed the way. I couldn't bear a re-route. I wanted to do it right, and feel right doing it.

Another time I saw an ant, a big black one, climbing across my windshield and flattening under speed. It was like watching a surveillance feed of a botched electric chair execution. It was uncensored war footage. Nope. It was nothing like that.

I could've used Gene, some backup, some distraction. He wouldn't come when called—sulking, I figured. I was sulking too, itchy and ready to go.

It was around that time Ken got back from his trip. I consented to seeing him. One night we went to see a movie about a man who couldn't remember anything. I couldn't tell if it was a horror or a comedy. Afterward we went to the diner like old times, only it had since been relocated. Previously it had been sitting on increasingly valuable land. Something about an historic registry: they'd moved the diner's original prefab shell a half-mile over, between a bank and a Mexican restaurant. They'd taken the occasion to add on.

Somehow, now, it was worse and smelled worse. Less clubhouse, more eating hall. On the plus, they'd kept those personal jukeboxes at each booth. One play for a quarter, three plays for two. No one ever used them, except kids and Ken.

"What is up with you?" he asked, sniffing and taking a big drink of water. I told him nothing. He asked for a quarter. I gave him one and he put on a pop song about one lover asking another lover not to leave. It should have seemed poignant but abandonment and wanting what you can no longer have, what you had once—that's rote stuff as far as pop and life are concerned.

"Fifty percent of pop songs are about someone leaving," I said. "And fifty percent are about how happy someone is to have someone."

Ken shrugged. I said I was just making an observation.

"What would you do if I left town?"

Ken's face dropped and cracked. "Like after everything is over?" He meant after Pop had died.

"Yeah, or whatever."

"I guess I'd want to go with you. We could have some kind

of big, life-changing time. Not Arkansas, though. Arkansas is horrible." Then, dragged into a charisma of complaint, he started in about how his mom had been up his ass to move down the whole time; how, yeah, the air was good there and his sister seemed to be doing a little better, but his cousins were a lot to deal with, and there wasn't any good coffee, and everyone there assumed he could speak Spanish and even though he could, he didn't like the presumption. People speak Spanish to you here, I said. All the time. Yeah, he said, but still. Years later I'd recall to Ken this moment. He'd groan at his young self and say grimly: "How eager I was to betray myself." And I'd think how shamefully unaware I was of any of Ken's reckonings, of anything beyond the reach of my own arms.

In the diner the song ended and our fries came, soggy in their red plastic baskets. They had been soggy on the old ceramic plates, too. Never fried long enough. Or the oil temp was low. Both or either. I wasn't hungry. The conversation didn't double back to leaving. I wasn't going to bring it up again.

THE NEXT DAY Ken left me a message about a party the next night, even though he knew I wouldn't go. "That is if you haven't left town yet," he joked. I thought maybe he was beginning to worry, that one day if he wasn't careful he'd look up and I'd be gone.

I used to think I was a person capable of anything. I don't mean this positively. Once Ken and I had broken into a mansion as teenagers. When I was sixteen, I didn't yet understand my circumstance. I didn't understand my family. My fixation was the homes in our neighborhood—the vinyl siding, the dandelions, a lack of sidewalk—and as I grew it became impossible not to snipe at those who had more. I don't mean this in a political way.

On one day a fair-skinned burnout named Macy had given Ken a joint in exchange for a lunch period with his completed Algebra II homework. To celebrate Ken and I decided to go on an adventure, or what passed for one in the suburbs.

It was not coincidence that we were both wearing black; we both wore a lot of black. We had reasoned it would make us less noticeable. Originally we'd planned to go pool-hopping in the local apartment complexes but the spring night had proven cold.

"What if—" I began, leaning against Ken, who was in turn leaning against the hood of his Buick, parked by my house under the shadows of a big false cherry tree. My parents had been asleep for hours. "What if we go over to Poplar Park and look in the windows?"

About one and a half miles from my family home was a new construction development of minor mansions. It was the next school district over and we knew no one; there no one knew us. Had Pop sold houses there it would've been a leg up. The families inside them coordinated with each other according to hobbies, not flaws.

Ken sucked air through his nose. "It's late."

"I'm bored," I said—that tatty siren call of the American teenager.

Without agreeing on anything, we began to walk in the approximate direction of the development. There were a few ghost-lighted windows, the occasional car rolling by and up to something. We made one turn, another, went down behind a row of townhouses, mud and gravel underfoot. A bird would startle and Ken would hiss "Shush," and then I'd laugh at him, and grab his shoulder to kiss it. "Nancy," I'd say, and then he'd shove me off sweetly. Beyond the townhouses was a four-lane road and we crossed it quickly as we would've in traffic. Though there was not one motor going this time of deep dead night.

Across an access road and along a marsh, our Chucks betrayed their weak seams. Our socks saturated. There were crickets making their own echoes, no other noise in the air.

As we approached the cul-de-sac we took a moment to look. There were three of the minor mansions in front of us. Each had a stone walk, a bay window, a wide deck on the backside visible from the front. But while two were set into a hill, the third, to our right, was set on a downward slope, which met that same marsh, only on the other side.

Pretending courage I led Ken behind that third mansion, billy-goating down a damp grass escarpment. The blinds were drawn, no sign of light. Soon we came to a small lower patio, beneath the deck, where there sat a small plaster water feature in the shape of an old-fashioned urn.

Where the patio met the house there was a sliding door backed by blinds. I wondered if it was unlocked. "Ken?" I asked. But he was over at the marsh line, pissing on some cattails. Even his urination, in its intimacy, was rousing. I will admit that when we were this age, or these ages—fifteen and sixteen and seventeen—I had a bit of romance in my heart. My parents were distant by sickness or disposition. In my own mind

I was a tenderfooted stray. Eventually my crush on Ken trans-
formed into a respectable family love. Which was convenient, as
one year later he would deliver the news that he preferred men.

As I waited for Ken to finish I daydreamt a proposition:
that we'd find a door unlocked. That it would slide open with
a beautiful silence. That we'd find ourselves in a staged rum-
pus room, with leather couches and a wet bar with an antiqued
mirror. That we'd go no further, but rather stretch like kittens
across the deep cushions. That I'd withdraw the joint surgically
from my fifth pocket, light it, and take a drag with the thumb
and forefinger like James Dean, who we loved then.

We would've gotten so high that our extremities felt like
masses of kind bees, floating us up just a few inches from the
earth. I, in my uncanny state, would move from my couch to his,
and be the little spoon. He would begin to stroke my hair, and I
would have pressed my butt deeper against his pelvis: the smallest aggression. And he would have started to kiss my jaw, and I,
so high I could hardly feel it happening, would have raised my
chin to kiss him on the mouth. We would have sent out our fingers like sentinels. We would have kept our clothes on; I would
have licked his cock through the crotch of his pants, where it
would smell silty, like the bottom of a creek. He would have
shifted himself upward until he was standing and then laid me
out on the mansion's basement carpet. I would have gone down
to greet it slowly, quietly humping the air in a way I would have
not yet known I could do. We would have fucked, with our
pants down, quiet at first, but then loud, taking turns finishing
the joint, feeling raw wetness between us. And in the oncoming

light we would have walked back to his car silently. We would have left the glass door open behind us, dreaming blissed out that the local raccoons and chipmunks and squirrels and turtles would, finding the door ajar, broach the alien edifice in waves.

We would not have been weird after; we would have joked about it. We wouldn't have waited on the future fumbling of relative strangers. We would have owned our sex differently.

I was not wrong that the back door might be unlocked; it was. I hissed Ken's name once more. He galloped from the marsh's edge and close together, we ventured in. The basement was standard issue: medium pile carpet, washer, dryer, an old couch, a coffee table with nothing on it. A weak lamp on a side table. The light being on, it keyed us up. We saw a door and I began to walk toward it. "What are you fucking doing?" Ken whispered.

I didn't answer him, only kept flat-footing it slowly across the carpet, until my hand was near the knob. The door was hung slightly crooked. When I pressed it with my open palm, it gave. Beyond, a bedroom with a desk and a bed, and in the bed, a sleeping person. On the walls, posters for rap-rock acts. A videogame system blinking and hooked to a television, spitting cables. Books and comics avalanched in one corner. Ken stood close behind me, his legs fit into the back of my knees, his chin ducked against my head. "Come on," he whispered wetly into my ear canal.

As we withdrew, something on the desk caught the wan light of the lamp. I pocketed it and did no examination until later when I was alone in my room. Now when I look at the hummingbird knife, my impulsive petty theft, I understand that the aftermaths of theft and sex can feel the same: a disassembling thrill.

I KEPT TRYING to leave town. Soon it was the end of September. Time was getting slim. To my landlord and to myself I had made what felt like a final pledge, an oath, solemn and straight lipped, that I'd be moving on. At the same time Ma had taken a leave of absence at work and had for now reduced the nurse's hours. Between escape attempts I went and saw my folks without looking at their faces or listening to what they said. I wanted to delay the reveal of my desertion. "I need you to go over this paperwork with me," Ma said one day, holding an envelope in midair.

"Tomorrow," I said. "I promise," I said. And got in my truck and drove back to my apartment to enter it one last time.

Each movement I made in the empty apartment jangled me. There was only one way to stop this. I packed my backpack with all my last minute things: wallet, keys, bottle of water, sunglasses, toothbrush, pain pills, that hummingbird knife, and another, more serious knife. I threw out all the condiments and took the trash to the tract dumpster. I whistled one note, locked the door behind me, and hopped to. I kept my house keys, for no matter the plan I was a true-blue wuss.

For a while, out on the road, everything was looking good. I felt—I don't know—clean for the first time in months. Directional as an arrow. In the left lane all the cars were moving in a liquid American way. I congratulated myself, aloud. "Denny!" I said. "By George, you've got it!" I hummed a bit and knocked out a little tune on the wheel. "Gene!" I hollered. He didn't show up. I felt sorry for myself, imagined him saying, "Denise, some things you've got to do on your ownsome-lonesome!" I wanted prayer beads. Rosary. A fortune cookie. Worry dolls. My friend! I was unfettered. Kept driving.

The clean boost didn't last long. I surveyed the traffic, feeling bright and calm, only to get cut off by a truck. I veered into the right lane. I measured my breathing. In front of me was a pickup just like mine. It was going slow, its bed jammed with split and stained upholstered castoffs. I eased up on the gas.

I couldn't see the driver, only the truck's junk. He was, I felt sure, someone my father's age. He would have married once or even three times, but, by plumbing or chance or choice, stayed childless. He would have seen a series of light industry jobs through enough years. He would have stopped asking after the names of wives and kids, or what anyone thought about the new highway project, or how the unions were doing. He would have grown quiet. I watched the truck's load carefully, watched the shadows on the back window of the cab shift when the driver jerked his head one way or another. I fell into a kind of spell.

Then his truck hit a bump and shimmied a couch half a foot to the right, so that I could see now the back of his browned neck. Presented with a body: here is a person I'd never know, I thought. It was an unaccountably sad thought, only because of its surprise and accuracy. I felt like a real schmuck when I felt tears on my cheeks. I had to pull the truck over. To be safe. I thought: I just need a day, half a day, to think out what I'm doing. So I turned back home with a wet face.

•

BACK IN STUDIO-SWEET-HOME my fingers discovered a
missed box of cereal tucked in the cupboard above the stove.
I ate up dry handfuls and lapped faucet water. By the evening I
started to feel wild and ready. I thought no more of endings or
beginnings. I knew I would leave now. It was only a question
of when. I slept on the dumb carpeted floor. In the morning
its rough pile woke me. My skin, pressed in it, had a gruff,
postparty texture. I still preferred wood. Being at home was
a retreat, but with an air of self-celebration. One more chance
to bon voyage. One more chance to remake a choice. "Gene?"
I called, groggy. He wasn't there to say hello or tell a story or
lambast me. I wondered had I run him off for good. I went back
to sleep with a smirk on my face.

At my second arousal I woke to observe my empty quarters,
the judging baldness I myself had fashioned. It was noon. Feeling bodily empty, I called for a pizza. When the man asked for
my address I teared up all over. Somehow I made it through the
order, and then waited like a patient, twiddling my flip phone.
When it rang, it was Ken on the line, asking if I was around.
"Still here!" I said, and invited myself over straightaway.

Forty minutes later I arrived at Ken's house with the pizza.
In his living room I patted his roommate's smelly mutt dog and
watched cable as Ken rolled out a sleeping bag. We sat on it and
nipped from a bottle of sour leftover party wine.

After half the bottle was gone he asked whether I was okay.
I asked him if I had to be. "We're all our own people, Den." I
could tell he was beginning to get tired of me; he hadn't asked

why I was there. This was one more reason to leave. He was his own person, I know and I knew, but at the time it was difficult not to think of him as a function of my own tragedy. It is cavalier and sinister to let something like this go on for very long.

Indeed an expression of exhaustion passed through Ken's features. It softened him from jaw to brow. I kicked the pizza box where it sat at the edge of our sleeping area. "Hey," he said. "There's no reason to be mean to the pizza." The smelly mutt dog, corn yellow, with eyes a similar color, farted and left the room. Ken pulled me across his lap like I was Jesus in some depressing contemporary pieta. He stroked my shoulder. I fell asleep and so did he.

We laid stiff and unmannered atop one another through the darkness. I woke periodically: greedily eating a slice of cold pizza above Ken's sleeping head, flipping the channels between infomercials and syndications, going to the bathroom. Somewhere around dawn I was up for good.

Ken snuffled into the blankets. The room was at last lighted, just. The corn-yellow mutt was up on my jaw, breath like old stew. I took my two hands and held his muzzle, whispered, "Listen!" His rheumy eyes orbited. He laid his big dog body beside my friend. "Goodbye!" I mouthed, and latched myself out of the scene.

FROM KEN'S I drove focused or blind. The goings-on of the morning stuck to the corners of my eyes. There was a child at a bus stop. There were newspapers thrown from a station wagon, a yield sign fallen over, a seasonal flag featuring daffodils wrapped over on itself and flush against a pole. There was a chow dog chained up in a driveway, an old man limping across a median, a silent church. The green and white signs hung dusty above the road. The highway greeted me, a gangway, a signal.

I made it out of the town limits, and then the county limits, and then the state's. There were reasons to turn back: the sights of a collapsing barn, an abandoned fruit stand, a closed RV dealership in the middle of nowhere stuffed to its gills with stock. I did not. It was my last week of paid-up rent, I reminded myself. I passed a backyard-sized cemetery and empty gas stations. The landscape was haunted with its own disuse.

I drove on in this long and languorous wheat-colored vacuum on its way toward gray, harvest nearly done. Leaving in late September wasn't the soul of smarts. Up on the mountain a frost would set in before I had a chance to enjoy the wild-flowers. I drove and whether I drove all night or many nights I couldn't say.

Time as perseverance.
Time as hunger. Time in
a natural way. Time when
you were six the day a
mountain. Mountain time.

ANNE CARSON,
from "Time Passes Time,"
Red Doc>

Going in one direction for so long, the final turn felt dramatic. It wasn't. I had a sweaty, crackling soda between my thighs. My temples hurt from squint. Only then did I realize I'd forgotten my sunglasses on Ken's coffee table.

Hocked off the highway and onto a long farm road, I drove past an operational gas station and a closed family restaurant and finally to the outfitter. It was a freestanding cinderblock building, flanked by drainage ditches. I parked. The lot was flyaway dirt and flyaway dust. When I got my feet on the ground my muscles felt like rotted rubber bands. I shook out the last drips in the soda bottle as I walked across the lot. The liquid made a scatter pattern in the dirt. Everything smelled like a bowl of dry grain, cut through with petroleum.

Once I got through the double doors I saw it was just like anywhere else: a place with stuff in it. By the entrance there was a bulletin board. Shooting ranges twelve miles away (indoor and outdoor, machine gun demos once every season), survivalist meeting groups (regional, all welcome), a litter of kittens in need of loving homes (calico). There was a handwritten sign for lawn services and handyman repairs, its fringed bottom curling with a repeated number.

Beyond the bulletin board there were a few racks of olive

clothes and orange clothes and black clothes. A shelf or two of boxes, crates full of varieties of one thing or another: compasses, carabiners, rope. The halftones of lures, and spools of line in half-lit fluorescents. A whole display of items useful in emergencies: water purification tablets, reflective blankets, an impressively small box of nutrient powders, flares, a waterproof map, a small bottle, a tent patching kit, crush-to-heat pouches. As if the right patent was all that was standing between a body and a painless, endless life.

There were boxes of waterproof boots lining the back of the store: more soldier, more savvy, than any part of my wardrobe had ever been. I touched a rough sleeve of a nearby jacket and felt a specific delight. I dined on the sights of these items. They pushed my brain full with the new anonymous, no room left for—

"Help you, miss?" In the dim light there was a skinny lady stood up behind the glass case of a firearms counter. She was pricing something, orange stickers clinging like burrs to her shirtsleeves. I told her I was supposed to be meeting someone, told her the man's name. "Do you know him?"

"Course," she said, then dialed and handed over the phone. Holding it reminded me of the one I'd left lodged between Ken's couch cushions.

When the man answered he said he needed an hour to get up there. "Be seeing you."

I held the phone over the gun counter. She retrieved it with her spindle arm.

"You the one staying up at EJ's cabin?"

"I am."

"How are you fixed for supplies?" she asked. Her salesperson smile was shallow and picketed.

I told her I was just fine, felt miffed she presumed otherwise. "You have a gun?"

"I'm an artist," I told her, sticking to my story. "Why would I need a gun?"

She said that you didn't know what you'd find up there, that a gal alone should supply herself with a bit of security.

I told her I had two knives, holding aloft my pretty hummingbird knife. She took it and extended the blade, looked down its axis and shuddered her head, tapped the glass counter quick. The reflected light licked her pitted cheeks.

Next I showed her my new carbon steel blade. On the back you could spark a fire with flint. "See?" I showed her how I wore the hummingbird knife on one side, on a climbing-grade carabiner, and the carbon knife in a leather-nylon holster on the other, like a fresh little professional.

She snorted. "It's up to you, of course." I didn't need the gun. But I wanted it.

The glass display whined as she unlocked it, slid it open, and handed over a gun. "This one's good for beginners," she said. "Ruger SR9. No safety, so you've got to shoot through the magazine before you put it down. Don't have to worry about how many bullets you've got left." She arrayed four boxes of ammunition. "Just in case you have to hunt, or practice a lot. Though this one's not for hunting." It was meant for concealed carry; one magazine held ten bullets, the other seventeen. "Keep the bigger one with you, and the smaller one in the piece."

I took the gun up in my hand. It was part plastic, like a toy. She showed me how to load the magazine, how to force my thumb down on the rounds, harder and harder as it filled. I did so with trouble. She clicked her lips and told me to keep pushing.

This woman, or the gun, gave me a risky feeling. I hadn't felt this way since high school, maybe, turning down the wrong hallway at lunch, coming upon the feral kids whose parents had never been around. But because of her association with the cabin owner, and her evident expertise, I presumed her to be well-meaning. My presumptions were crisp and quick.

"You want to see how it handles?"

We went out the back through the storeroom, stood in the midday sun at the bottom of a grass-seed hill. There were pines and poplars cut back into a crescent, a quick chill wind slicing through the heat, snapped stalks in a far field. The target was a drawing of a hefty man in blue, gun drawn, an old-style mob bagman, clipped to a cardboard A-frame, weighted. The clouds above us looked matted.

"Never point a loaded gun at anything you wouldn't shoot," the skinny lady recited. Like she was doing an impression of herself or maybe someone she'd seen on TV.

I missed and missed and the sound of that was like a gigantic book falling. A wall falling. Excuse me: a gravestone falling on hard marble. "The kickback is almost nothing," I said, and she said, half-lidded: "Yep."

Once I stopped staring at her and got my eye on the target I hit once, missed once, hit twice: jawbone, armpit, crotch. Slowly the gun began to feel as small as it was. I shot a few more times, deciding. I began to feel in myself a new warlike way. This was a fiction but I still shot and shot. At last the skinny lady interrupted the rhythm.

"Fine," she said. "Guess that's enough," as if she'd remembered who I was to her, which was no one. Inside she sold me the gun for three of my last four hundred-dollar bills. It felt dangerous to have so little cash. But there was nothing to buy on the mountain. I asked her if I needed permit paperwork. She laughed, said not to worry, turned, didn't turn back.

Armed, I went out to the truck and unfolded my inventory list from the glove box. I worked the car, elbowing boxes and prying plastic tubs, till I was sure everything was there. It was a motley mix, based on manuals, prepper forums, and other online hearsays. I guess I could've spent more time figuring out what would be of use and what wouldn't. But that didn't interest me at the time.

I added the gun and rounds to the list and slid it unloaded into my backpack, whose seams I had double-basted—every one, in a shit way, but done—with a curved needle long as my pinky. Every button on every shirt had been triple-sewn. I lay down on the pickup bench with my knees up, hands over my heart, looking at the low clouds. I ignored for no good reason the seatbelt stay nudging my ribs sharply. I could have moved but fell asleep instead.

A minute or an hour later I heard a knock on the window. This was the beginning of untracked time. Upside down a man in a baseball cap was at my driver side window and grinning: a white broom moustache, ear hair. I got a flighty thrum-thrum in my chest but opened the door anyway.

The man asked was I Denny who he spoke with on the phone. I said yes I'm Denny who he spoke with on the phone. "You shift on over," Earl John said. "It'll be easier." I opened the driver side door. He was wearing overalls, the quilted kind, sweaty looking in this early autumn heat. "I'll be happy to keep your truck down at my place," he said as we drove away from the outfitter. "Long as you don't need it." I was now passenger to this stranger, and also passenger to my own dumb desires.

I watched him drive with confidence. He looked like I don't know what kind of man. He turned down a smaller road and up a wider road. Then, troubling gravity, we switchbacked up the steep side of a mountain.

The tree cover got taller and taller, in every green. I reminded myself that the leaves would turn soon. As soon as I did I saw a flame orange maple. I reminded myself that nothing was an omen.

We passed a pocketful of deer in the darkening branches. When I exclaimed Earl John laughed. "You see many deer where you are?" he asked.

I did not here recall the "cuts of ruined game" on the street the day I had learned of the cancer's return. I was not yet in the position of making my story. Rather I was riding headlong into this new life. "Yes," I answered. "But there's no room for them anymore."

"You know they did that controlled shooting down south of here. A deer can be really fatal, you know. For whatever reason, you'll see, there aren't too many deer hanging out right around the cabin. Or you won't see. The deer at least."

I didn't laugh, but asked: "You ever actually licked a salt lick?" It was something I had read about in one of the books, something you could use to attract deer. I imagined it was simply a block of salt—it was not; I imagined it a mineral tongue amusement. Beside the road, ferns batted like lashes.

Earl John murmured in the negative and we drove on. I couldn't think of anything else to say. Or, I thought that anything I said could betray me, and what if he was the one, now that I was almost there, to turn me back.

I wondered briefly was Earl John another figment. No—he was a human, apart from me. I felt a draining. And then realized I must be psychically exhausted, scrambled—no longer able to digest that which was there plainly.

"What?" Earl John said. I told him I hadn't said a thing.

In the late sun the wilderness was gilded. I let it build a little joy in my chest. I rubbed the holster of my carbon steel blade and then the beak of my hummingbird knife, and shuffled my legs back and forth in the passenger well, humming a tune I only sort of remembered, or thought of doing so.

At last we came to a large field and at the end of it was something I'd been told was Earl John's lake plane, there on its outsize water skis, there bereft on a strip of dirt cutting through the thick yellow grass. Earl John pulled the truck up beside it. I was alone with a real stranger in a place unknown to me. Denise, I thought to myself formally—Denise, this is almost nearly what you've wanted.

"Here," Earl John said. We began in tandem to unload the truck. I was holding a plastic tub at my groin, shoulder blades tensed, when he looked at me sternly but not without politesse. "Let me do this packing," he said. "It's all about the balance." And so I handed off my carefully accrued wares to this stranger who was about to take us up, into pure air. Without a thing to do I fiddled my boot along the top of the grasses. A fly or other insect presented its curiosity by landing midway up my laces. "I don't know you," I said to it softly. In response it buzzed off.

In the cab Earl John fastened me to my seat. He checked his instruments as I rubbed my chest where the seat belt strapped it. I was given a pair of battered headphones. I put them on and soon we went up. The plane shook. We flew low. *Here* was now *down there. Heart* was now *stomach*.

And the down there, what a there it was. I didn't feel free but I did note then that the world seemed to be presenting itself. The spines and poufs and slanted facets of trees and rocks and water. Then homes with extensive decks. Then chipped-roof houses. Then no houses. Then nothing but the whitening afternoon sky, and the green and green and brown and brown, and the blue black of some water nipping at shores. The plane belly flopped in air pockets. My own belly went with it. My mouth stayed closed.

Once at the local strawberry festival I had gone up in a prop plane with Pop, my first flight. The prop plane had not gone very far up nor been there for very long. Woozily, we'd disembarked and from a stall procured strawberry shortcake made with pound cake from the Giant, taken large anchoring bites. We stood by a Mary Kay–pink Cadillac while I told Ma, who had declined the ride, about my first trip up. "Eat your dessert," she'd directed, looking somewhere else.

Years later, we'd all flown commercial to California to spend time with Ma's surviving family: cousins who affected breeziness, and who wore natural fabrics in generous cuts and had diets based on their moods and skin. In meeting them I thought how I didn't need more family; I hadn't been raised to have such specific preferences. The flights themselves, out and back, had not been notable.

Earl John started the decline. The cabin filled with fuzzy noise. Or it had been there from the start. Through the windshield I saw on the horizon a kind of lookout tower. Sight soon blurred. One sense was drowning out another, a thought drowning out a feeling, a feeling drowning out a thought, the water coming up and flapping and spraying beneath us as we alighted on a lake between two mountainsides. My eyes gulped. I felt like an air-popped kernel coming finally to rest. I pulled the two halves of my ponytail tight.

EARL JOHN LASHED the plane like a boat to a small dock. It rocked there in the lake water; I was in a new life where a plane was equal to a boat. In this new life what dwelt in sky could do well enough in water. Earl John was next to me, pilot headphones around his neck. "Take whatever you want this trip. We'll have to come back anyways."

I strapped on my backpack, snatched an overstuffed tub, and followed him over the land, which was open and precious. "Everything'll be safe sitting there?" I asked.

"There's no one around here, much," he said. "Unless they're coming to you." He told me there was a state park twelve or fifteen miles up the road. But another thirty to the nearest trail, so—don't worry, he said—I wouldn't be bothered. I wondered if I was worried about being bothered; I didn't care much what would happen to me.

We worked through a small sash of woods. Even on the cleared path, branches snapped at my sides. The top of the tub was troublemaking, working its way from the fasteners and pinching my palms. These woods weren't that deep, but rather just deep enough to have seemed deeper: thirty feet through, and then out. We cut across a dry blonde meadow. At my knees and ankles I could feel bugs or errant hairs. Either way I felt buzzed. Perhaps it was the altitude.

My hip flexors see'd and sawed. I gritted my teeth. I could be whip, cart, and mule. I tried to look happy doing it. The meadow grasses and stalks waved, then gave up to a small stand of deciduous trees. The man made a belching, trying noise. A moment after, we were in a clearing, at the cabin. I pressed my feet up its four broad, bowed steps and launched my burden across the porch.

"Easy girl," Earl John said. "You're home now."

"Great," I said, straightening. My cheeks felt stretched thin. I realized then I was smiling and had been for quite some time.

The cabin was a simple house, with a wood shingled roof. It had a front porch that was a good place to imagine lounging. I wondered whether lounging was allowed in the wilderness. I wondered if I could be a person who lounged.

In the clearing yard, there was packed dirt with patches of grass. There was a fire circle made with an old metal ring. Beside

the cabin was a large and orderly pile of wood. A bug flew up
my nostril and I scratched my nose until it became embarrassing. Another bug climbed against my hairline. Gray-gold light
fell over the whole mountain; my ears popped. A bug climbed
in there too. Then I was shaking my head up and down, ear to
earth. Earl John didn't notice.

"Me and my wife used to come here for vacations when we
were first married," he said as he unlocked the bolt; with his
shoulder he butted open the sticky door. People are always of-
fering me their lives; it's always been this way. Despite my many
faults I have an open face. I am naturally good at "placid," if not
placidity, "patient," if not patience. "The kid though didn't seem
interested."

"Kids!" I said too loudly. He didn't comment. I let myself
go quiet. The place was hazy inside, except for the floody, glowy
light melting through the window seams. I saw that the front
room was wide, with a wood plank floor, a pullout sofa and
chair at one end, a utility sink and counter on the other. By the
front windows was a big cream linoleum table that could dine
eight, except it was pushed up against a corner and only had four
chairs. I thought then that I'd rotate between the chairs for each
meal, so that none felt wasted; meanwhile Earl John spoke of the
well he had dug, its idiosyncrasies. He told me there was a stash
of junk drawer stuff—TP and tools, some backup kitchen items,
things other renters had left—under the bunk. "Oh, and burn
the trash you can. The other stuff you can save to bring back."

"I'll bring it back," I said emptily, looking at the little ripple
of the floor planks. All I wanted to do was lay my body across

it. My stomach hurt from the plane ride and my chest hurt from what I was doing there. Then I became taut and bloated and cold, changeable as the weather, just like a woman. I was ready to be alone and not lonely.

"You know how to use this stove?" he asked. I made a non-committal noise and so he gave me a provisional tour. Squat as an old TV, it was lacquered black with a hinged door in its front. A thick shaft came out its back, then chimneyed through the roof. "This is the flue, gotta make sure this is open. And here's where you put in your logs and kindling and tinder. Make sure you lock this so the house doesn't get all full of ash, mind. And up here is where you can cook what you like."

What did I look like, what did my face look like, when he asked could I build a fire. "I've built some fires," I said.

"You are going to get good at it, little miss." I sneered to myself; the idea of learning anything seemed at this juncture ludicrous. But seeing my face he only chuckled—a dab of chiding pity perhaps—then showed me the rest of the house. There were bunk beds in back, adult sized. The bottom bunk had a full-size mattress jutting. There was a bathroom sink and a vinyl cubicle with a hose you could set up on a hook for a shower.

Out the back door and down three steps, a little way into where the woods crept up, was an outhouse with a crescent moon cut out of the purple-painted door. "Wife was good with a jigsaw," he explained. Beyond there was an old fence that must've once divided carefully the cabin's territory from the surrounding wild, though now it was falling down.

Earl John led me back to the lakeshore so we could

finish hauling my supplies. I murmured and followed him back through the meadow, with little interest in returning to any-where I'd been previously.

THE SUN WAS down by the time we were done unpacking the seaplane. A lantern was on. Candles were lit. I located a small flashlight and put it in my pocket. All of a sudden it was romantic. Was it the light or the place or us. Nope: I was demented, pried open. I looked to Earl John and he said thanks and I said thanks and he seemed almost sorry to be leaving me there. He had, I noticed, an involuntary eye twitch. I felt a little bit sorry for myself too. With the darkness I was understanding things—my new hang—a hair more.

Earl John began to say goodbye, that he'd meet me back up here the following summer as agreed. I did not have any plan to live that long. I did not really have any plan. He looked at my face. I wondered was I grimacing or melting. I was making myself obvious, certainly. For after looking in my face, my ob-viously unplanned face, Earl John turned to give me a half hug.

"Do you have headlights on that thing?" I asked. He laughed and said yes, that he'd get off and back fine, long as he didn't have to land in the water, which he didn't. What if I undid his overalls, I thought, though I didn't move. We exist with sets of stories or lists: the ways we must feel during loss or solitude, the ways we must present the self to others, the ways we must act. But there are other and scarier ways to be.

Earl John seemed heavier than he looked, not lighter. His overall fasteners were not the usual slide-to-button but something more complicated. In him there were weighty things, or so I assumed. Wistfulness. The wild. Big game opponents. Those overalls! I was staring.

"Noticing these?" he said. He gestured to his bib.

"They look serious."

"They are. You got anything like them?"

I looked at my pile of stuff in the wan light. It was ignorance made material. I shook my head. Then he began to disrobe.

"I'll confess," he said, as he sat down on the couch, undoing his bootlaces. "I only have sons, but I still feel like some kind of bad dad leaving you up here alone."

"I'll be okay," I said, slowly. It was like watching a soap bubble in air, watching this happen to me. This feeling of unhappening, of about-to-be, nested itself inside me, has never left.

"No, I'm serious," Earl John said. "You seem responsible enough, like you can take care of yourself, what do you say, street-smart. My son the computer programmer could use some of that."

"Thank you," I said quietly as Earl John wrested his boot from his foot. I watched as he rose, sock footed, and began to unfasten his overall straps, those which had seemed to me previously un-unfastenable. Beneath he was wearing a button-down denim shirt. He let the straps fall and started a strange shimmy, his jowls jiggling a bit, so little I wouldn't have noticed if I weren't me, there in that remote cabin, living it. The bib fell down like a broad tongue. He unfastened more fasteners at the waist, on either side.

In respect or in embarrassment I looked away, to the corners

of the room, their small pockets of dust and webs. A thoop-
plunk noise came from the direction of the man. It was his overalls, now sitting at his ankles. I saw then that he was wearing
thin jeans beneath, the color of cataracts. "Oh!" I breathed, in-
voluntarily, then realized he had been talking the whole time.

"—it's not that he doesn't have friends, but I think they're
all over the internet, and that's all fine, but I do wonder what it's
doing to him, not having anyone to, I don't know, cat around
with, go to things with. He doesn't get along with Janey's son
either. I hoped he would. Can't blame them."

"But you just said he had friends?" I managed.

"Yeah, but not real ones," he said, sitting on the couch, folding the overalls. I watched him put his boots back on, the laces
pulling tight.

"But if they're real to him?" Well of course I was thinking of Gene, 100 percent less real, 100 percent more annoying.
I wanted verification that he was gone or not gone. Would he
loiter and sting me here with no end but my own demise.

"You sound just like him," he said and laughed thinly. "I
guess it's a different world now. My stepson on the other hand,
he isn't a type who needs—" He stopped.

I looked around, watching finally as he folded the overalls
and held them out to me. "I couldn't."

"I think you have to," he said. "Just wait until winter. I
know they'll be big on you but that's all the more room to layer.
You'll be happy to have them."

I took them, thanked him. I felt like I was letting go of
plumb weights, as I laid them carefully on the sofa's arm.

"Now tell me if you really know how to build a fire?"

I did, in theory. But theory didn't manage much out there, so I shook my head. In the stove he crossed a few large logs. Then he added some sticks and paper and lit a match. Right off the paper blazed, smoking. After some damp resistance, the logs caught too. Slowly the house warmed.

"You'll be okay," he said. For me, "okay" was a familiar expectation. This was folly on everyone's part. Earl John side-hugged me goodbye once more. It was not a notable departure, except that he was the last live person I planned or expected to see. It seemed impossible I'd survive the week.

As I was waving from the front porch, watching his flash-light beam swipe out of view, through the stand of trees and somewhere down into the blonde meadow, I was thinking: oh, you old goat, just leave already!

But I didn't mean it. Back inside I rolled out my sleeping bag across that plank floor, got a glass of water, thought of the purple-doored latrine and then thought better of it, locked the door bolt, and got down into the bag. The ceiling in the cabin was low but some eye-brain trick made it look as if it was reced-ing. I was hungry but my heavy head won.

Much later, I think, I woke to see the fire in smolder. My heart was bellows fast. If it's now I die, I thought, well, then—all the better. But instead it was the fire that died. The warm smoke kicked out of the stove in thin curls. My heart slowed. I shimmied deeper into the bag and fell asleep again like I didn't even hear the crickets loud as ravens.

•

THAT FIRST MORNING I woke to feel mummified. It was hot in the cabin and close; by the front window, in the sunbeams, little jerk flies kibitzed. They moved not like doves, but like chickens in air.

I sensed it was late in the day. Snot corked my nostrils. I wondered again about Gene. When had I seen him last? Not since our exotic real estate encounter in the empty apartment. Had he forgotten himself? It seemed possible or probable he wouldn't return. So I moved him from my worries: a single block lifted from an avalanching pile.

With no responsibility to be a person, I found I was bored. The day was undetermined and indeterminate. I was being a brat. I decided to eat something. The drawback of solitude is boredom, is an excess of agency, is yourself.

To loosen neck muscles I swung my head. I shook myself out like a blanket. I let out a bellow and thought: it's a berry-blast kind of morning! The meal-replacement bars were in one of the tubs. I knew which one. This made me feel clever.

Nakedly I took chomps of the bar, then swallowed. The trick, I thought, is to make a schedule. Or the trick is to have small goals. Or maybe the trick is to do whatever I want. But it didn't matter if I was bored. Surely I would succumb to an infection or fall or animal attack; I wouldn't have to be bored forever. In the meantime I vamped about it.

I held the bar out and away from me. The wrapper, with its zoomy design and print, was too heavy with hands, with personages. In magenta silhouette, a miniature woman leapt from an inch-high cliff with a paragliding rig. I dropped the bar on my beloved floor. The sound was sapless.

Meanwhile my armpits were spouting sweat rivulets. When I touched them, experimentally, I felt sick of myself. It was time to go swimming. This was one small goal.

Outside I heard a faint falling noise. I went to the window to see what I could see. There was no living thing in evidence beyond the front curtains, in the daylight. I thought how the indoors were a smaller fraction of my life now. Pursuantly the outdoors made promises.

I finished the bar and dressed carefully in my khakis and a T-shirt, rubbed my skin all over with DEET-based spray, bent beneath the kitchen spigot and got some water across the roses in my cheeks. The water was shuddery and silty but no matter. I put on my untied boots and strode. Outside the air was gently warm, tea left to cool.

The land looked different than it had when I'd been yoked with my possessions. Now it stretched and bounded. On the horizon line, just closer than the mountain peaks was some kind of tower with a trussed base and flat-roofed volume atop. I had seen it from the air. I could not determine how far it was, or whether it was being used currently. I looked across the broad blonde meadow, seeing how the path ahead knit itself into the trees. The woods were both deciduous and evergreen, needles and dry leaves and fallen branch arms covering the ground, accompanied by low green brambles and whispery ferns of at least nine varieties. Their leaves were different from one another at

least. I saw a squirrel, and several birds overhead. I felt a bit like
a squirrel, found in a scrubby backyard or on a mountain just
as easily. Context did not change our watchfulness, our impreci-
sion; our insignificant, rattley chitter.

I went on walking and surveying. Soon the woods broke
open again. I came upon the lake and its plank dock. The night
prior it'd seemed so far from the cabin. Or what I mean is: It
wasn't very far to the lake from the cabin. A heavy load makes
a longer road, or something like that.

By the lake the air was flat. Before this I would never have
described air as flat. There was a bitten-feeling on my ankle's
dry skin. I was nervous about the lake and going in it, though
I loved to swim. I preferred pools: water with no secrets. But,
goodbye, pools! I thought. I was not in pool-land anymore. This
lake was a stranger. I wondered about leeches.

I took off my boots, my shirt and pants, folded them beside
me. I tried not to think of snakes. Lying down on the dock I
felt spreading and heavy. Like a piece of dough waiting to rise.
Without Gene I found myself more aware of my performances,
my roles, the way I played to a nonexistent camera.

Above me the sky was wide. Here I have all the world,
I thought, when once I had so little. A studio apartment, the
shut-in life of automobile transportation, various rooms in other
people's homes, the balance-beam corridors at work, the little
closets where I fed my flies. The freed flies who were by now
surely dead. Here in the wild I had every option of movement
and space, a self-serving roamer's delight.

Once the sun was high and I could see it like an opponent, I rose from the dock and slipped into the water. There it was: the untrustworthy lacey, mossy life of the lake's bottom. I made circular laps around the water's edge, staying away from the deepening center. I felt permitted to expend energy, at last. All that time in the suburbs I had been holding on to it: just in case, just waiting, just ready. My strokes started sloppy and then smoothed as I tensed. I extended my limbs and rode my own current. With my eyes closed I cut forward, then flipped onto my back and floated, at last opening my eyes to a dense stand of squat trees. There was a large water bird resting itself on the far end of lake, some kind of heron. Its neck kinked and straightened, and then the bird set off, over me and the trees. I waved goodbye.

There seemed to be an especial peace in any water. I used to swim with Pop in pools, after the first cancer and before the second. At the time of us swimming together I was first a freshman living in the dorms at the university, then a sophomore who lived at home, and so on. Usually Mondays, always Tuesdays, definitely Wednesdays, sometimes Thursdays, I'd set my alarm for too early, wake to roll on my Speedo and cover it with a T-shirt or sweatshirt, along with soccer shorts, then report for duty at the door. Pop wore sweatpants, a shirt, a windbreaker if it was chilly. Our suburban air was apple-crisp. The streets were empty, except for a sighing bus making its way down the main drag.

Pop drove us to the municipal, where at the front desk we said hi to the gal, grabbed towels, descended to the locker rooms to be gender-sorted, and then reunited on the green-tile pool deck, where it smelled like chlorine with a secret of mildew. The tall windows along the length of the water showed wet grass, or melting snow, or blotting sun. If we were too early, a lifeguard would be in the water unspooling the lane lines, and if they were, we'd get in and help. If not I'd sit on the edge while Pop used the ladder to lower himself in. He'd stretch in the shallow end. I'd ignore his body—so lately sick—in favor of the lane line clicks and flip-flop slaps echoing. I never stretched, got started right away.

Pop had a foot on me in height, but he was messy. I had a handsome crawl, and often clocked him speed-wise. When you're swimming you have to keep your head down; you have to stretch your arms like a ballerina; you have to rotate into your stroke; you can't forget about your legs. Everyone forgets about their legs. Does a dolphin forget their tail? My flip-turns were shoddy however—I always ended up with water up my nose, a chemical soda. I did them anyway. They cut down on time. Speed had been important to me.

We'd do thirty laps, 1,500 meters, because we said we would. In the water I would think about the number of each lap as I stroked, repeated it to myself over and over. Twenty-three, twenty-three, twenty-three, twenty-three; until it was time for twenty-four, twenty-four, twenty-four, twenty-four. Twenty-five, twenty-five, twenty-five. Up to thirty and I'd hit the wall huffing and shining. When I was done usually Pop had a lap or two to go.

Later in the locker room I'd stand under the shower's faint warm trickle, feel it saturating my suit. I'd wash my hair with hand soap from the dispenser. Then I'd dry off again and put my hair up and dress and buy a can of pineapple-orange juice from the Minute Maid machine for Pop and me to split. We'd alternate sips on the way home; sometimes I'd drive if Pop felt tired; the juice was sun + metal = hello, day! Often I wondered were we being stubborn, trying to unmark orange juice's sinister associations, trying to evict "It's not the bad kind" from our psychic rooms. The new context worked, mostly. Only briefly, if ever, did I recall during those car rides pulp congregating brightly at the tops of glasses. When I did I found I could look out the car window, scumble it away. Ma would be up by the time we returned. She would kiss our cheeks and ask airily if we had a good swim.

Later, in my first morning class, I'd let my hair down. It dried faster that way. It would release the smells of the pool, the chlorine and mildew and hotel-smelling hand soap. Once a tall fellow student—having smelled me, I suppose—asked if I was serious about swimming. Did I want to join the intramural team. Bet it's obvious what I said, never once looking at his face.

Between my graduation and the mountain, our swimming outings ceased. First I stopped, saying I was too busy, though I was not. Then Pop stopped, sick; started again, then stopped, sick again. In this ignorant, organic way we began to abandon one another.

When was the first last time I saw Pop. He was judging the cream in his tea. He was hitting the back of the spoon on the countertop. He was vertical, which, by that time, was uncommon. "Do you want a cookie maybe?" I had asked him. He had looked good for fifty-five; his thinning body passed for cosmopolitan. The cookies were lemon wafers: a kind he liked. I can't remember what his answer was. I can no longer remember. Then I did what we all do: I left through a door. I got in a car. I drove.

Now tired, I withdrew from the lake and made my way for the woods. Drenched from swimming and regret I found I wanted for Gene. It was such a drab, obvious equation: one I could not help solving. I was lonely. I sneezed as I dried. I wanted to bare my teeth at someone. I wanted to dig my fingers into his eye sockets. I wanted to punish the old man for the crime of being me.

I sneezed again, and looked out to the landscape for his silhouette. I found nothing, except: there was a squirrel, and another, at the edge of the meadow. Beyond there was something larger and slower and darker than a squirrel, or a shadow. And, birds! Then there again the dark shadow flipping in and out of my peripheral vision. I turned to see what looked like a small furred mammal, disappearing into the edge of the woods, brown or black.

In my hurry, I hadn't remembered to be scared of the non-human beings in my new ecosystem. Having the gun, which sat in its bandanna back at the cabin, meant not a thing. The mammal made a switch-thump-switch in the thickets of brambles and trees. The new near prospect of death made me for a moment a straight-A student. I mean: I resolved to be more careful, more observant of my surroundings. I resolved to try and do research in my books. I resolved not to be eaten by a bear, nor bitten open by a slightly smaller thing disinterested in consuming me. I resolved not to watch such a wound infect and yellow, also resolved to begin target practice posthaste. Fear outstripped any cavalier feeling regarding my fate. I stood still until I could no longer hear the thing in the woods, then walked back gingerly.

The nature of nature is mystery, I reminded myself. Or it is like this down-mountain. There, beyond weather and bug bites, it's largely illegible. Between nature and the gaze, gauze. Between modern humans and the natural world, a scrim. But now we were together in the blonde meadow: nature and I. A new romance. Or, a sweaty intimacy, the sort I could then handle.

LATER BACK AT the cabin I started a fire, wished and breathed on it. I started some soup, and read. I was on the blade of wanting to find any animal, any big animal, for a challenge and a ceding to some gore. Though the Boy Scouts book promised that it was a "complete encyclopedia of wilderness living," it carried only a little section about backing away from predators, never running or challenging. There was a longer passage on currying your pack camel, by which they meant brushing, not cooking.

My other survival book—written by two companionable oldsters and published in the early 1970s—noted unhelpfully that "the ordinary farm bull" was the most dangerous animal in the world, and not to worry about wolves and coyotes, bobcats, mountain lions, bears, nor something called a javelina. It was a wild hog, they said. I wondered was it *jave-a-lina* or *have-a-lina*, if it used a Spanish pronunciation. I remembered then Ken complaining about people speaking Spanish to him in Arkansas and sensed in myself a new and hollow cruelty. By being here and not there I would not only leapfrog Pop's expiration, but also Ma's, and Ken's living and dying, missing the continual birthing and unfolding and decaying of the world. This cruelty was not unpleasant to feel; it was only news.

I got up and stirred the thickening soup and then when it seemed ready put the pot on a clay trivet the shape of a sun which was sitting on the table so smartly. I imagined Earl John's old wife had selected it. The moon of the outhouse. The sun of the kitchen. Once the soup had cooled I gulped it. Full, I sat for a sec. Then I got ready for my next preservative chore: to practice, to take aim. Now that I had a firearm I would be able, I figured, to choose the moments of folly and those of defense. Fate is not a thing. But a gun is. I ate more soup.

When I finished I took the gun from its bandanna-wrap deep in the innards of my backpack, and revealed it to my-self. Its sheen marketed something unclear. I remembered the skinny lady's warning, her eyes wrung out from something like old loss. When looking for someone to show you how to respect a firearm, find a reformed junkie or career mourner. Find a sad queen of gun sales, in rural parts unknown. This is inaccurate and sentimental adornment. I was holding a gun. The bigger magazine stayed nestled in the pack: It was more than what I required.

Once more I wished Gene were there. He had shot far more than me, I gathered. With movie stars and dogs or fellow pilots or his pa or maybe even Marjorie. He was the part of me who had bullish confidence, and an aptitude for killing things: No wonder he was gone. I was scared on this mountain but it was a manageable fear. I would not admit it past my doorways. Gene had eaten what he had hunted, after posing with it for pictures, I imagined. On the other hand I got queasy when I thought too hard about steak or even eggs.

Though I did not have any wish to eat game, that is, an animal I had shot—or even pose with it—I did want to be able to defend myself if necessary. So what would I do with a carcass? I would leave it to rot as a sign to all other potential carcasses, let the ill maggots and munchers come, warning: look here, do not challenge this wild woman of the valley. She will allow your body, dead, to undo itself without majesty or respect.

OUT BACK BEYOND the latrine there was a remnant of weathered wood fence, about fifteen feet long and four feet tall, and against it grew late pink blossoms, leggy and darting in the breeze. I zoomed at those petals. They felt like the right target. With not a little trouble, I loaded the clip as the skinny lady had shown me. I listened for the mammal but all I heard was chirps and caws from birds in the tree tops. I watched the blossoms bob.

Finally, finally, Gene appeared, sitting on the fence a good length down. My own brain had at last bestowed a mercy. "Don't aim that thing at me," he said all bratty.

"—the fuck have you been?" I asked.

"Busy," he began. His voice was more tattered than usual. His eyes looked unfocused, as if he were drunk or ill. "You're not my only charge." He dismounted the fence and then slumped upon it, waving his hand at bugs. "Git!" he squealed. He was a sputtering irritant of a man. Had he been this way all along. I wondered was he sinking further out of sight.

At this I felt nauseous, and held up the gun. "Look what I got!"

"A toy?" he laughed.

"A toy what'll kill ya."

"Oh, well!" He straightened and curtsied at me. "You know you could use a Lucie, some hound to fetch your kills."

"I'm just doing some target practice." I made an impatient back-of-throat *uch*. So recently I had been wanting Gene. Now I felt like this. I didn't know then it was a common condition—to want something, to get it, and then to regret getting it. I didn't know it was usual to be annoyed at your own wants.

"When I first got her she liked to clomp down on the kill. But I trained her out of it. Now let me see what you can do with that hunka junk."

I nodded. The gun felt smooth in my hand. I was no longer scared. Now there was no variance between who I was to the world and who I was to myself. Boldly I raised the gun and pointed it one-handed at the blooms, then lowered it to the stems, remembering the way the kickback could warp an aim. Then I lowered it and took a breath. Gene was now standing beside me, watching. "Not bad for a girl! You look almost natural."

"Not bad for anyone, you dolt." I seethed glamorously. A bug bite on my wrist was making a little siren up my nerves but I ignored it, pushing back my shoulders like Ma had always wanted me to. A ladylike posture. I raised the gun, brought up my left hand, stabilized myself, and squeezed.

The kickback was just a light shove. The bullet thunked, taking a rude bit from the gray rotted fence. I stood hefting my breath as in reps. The latrine let loose a low shit scent on the breeze. Gene had walked over to the cabin's back stoop to

rub his temples and miserate under his breath. I watched the
birds in retreat against the sky, sprinting jerkily. The fence as-
ters waved as if underwater. "You know about mouthing?"

"Mouthy? Like you?" I said.

"No. Like you gotta give the hunting dogs a taste of the kill
before you take it from them. The dogs track the scent, they tree
the thing, you shoot it, then you gotta give them some satisfaction, so you let 'em snap at it a bit."

"That's normal?" I asked. He nodded. It seemed, simultaneously, uncouth and logical. I wondered what movie, what
person, what book had seeded this info, what lie, what stray
scrap of eavesdrop. His face screwed and unscrewed, lively as a
propeller in the wind. "What you gotta do is take the fruit out of
the pan before it burns on account of the sugar," he said.

"What?"

He coughed and said sharply, "Never you mind!" He was
back on his scramble.

I resumed; I raised the gun again, squeezed, hit nothing.

Squeezed it again, hit nothing.

A dead branch screeched behind me. My stomach sloshed
itself full of acid. I thought, maybe this is enough for now.
Maybe I'm a wuss.

Then I remembered how the skinny lady had told me not to
put down the gun till it was unloaded. I had more shots to go.

So I did it again, raised and squeezed, squeezed again. The
flowers bobbed, pink as porno labia.

Again, again.

Then the petals were gone, a whole bloom gone, a whole

stem broken and doubled over the fence. "Woo hoo!" I yelled
with a full throat into the sweet air. "Yee haw!"

Gene laughed in a single huff then began to meander along
a row of brambles stage left. "Atta girl," he said. "I suppose."

By my casual math I had one more bullet, one or two. My
heart was fast, turned on. All I wanted to do was eat and fuck.
A steak? I'd eat it raw. In compensation to myself, steak-less, I
decided I'd hit the fence, give it something to remember me by,
then go home and tend to myself.

My stomach rippled and laced with energy. I raised the gun
in a messy kiddie pose and squeezed that trigger till the kickback. A real whammo. The last bullet bit the fence good.

Then, sassy, I did it again—just for funsies. Just for the
feeling.

Except, as is always true in public service announcements:
guns are unpredictable. The last bullet hadn't been the last bullet. It was instead penultimate. And when, unexpectedly, I let
out that real last-last bullet, it whiffed under the last cross post
of the fence and fast and far to who knew.

Then all at once, it came—the noise to spoil a party: a baby's
shocked yelp. A baby wailing. A baby howling purple, indigo,
maroon. I looked around for Gene, but he had his back to me
and seemed to be breathing heavily. I wondered then was he dying too, wondered then at the fiendishness of my imagination.
Then I remembered the yelp.

I may be a cold customer, but I'm not heartless. So soon as I
heard that cry I knew I'd have to ferret it out. I laid the gun on
the ground by the fence post. My limbs were full of cold pins as

I scaled the fence in a one-two swing and began to crash farther away from the cabin and into the deeper woods. As I ran—for I realized then I was running—I let the branches snap me in the face, brambles knot and then tear at my feet. The wail ripped and ripped and ripped the air as I ran and ran and ran.

And then it stopped.

I was deep into the forest by then, and I turned about, looking for any sign. As the adrenaline soured I thought, is this just another Gene-type scenario? Was I letting myself go mad, or, well, I mean, madder? Lock elbowed, I used my arm to brace myself vertically against a trunk. I surveyed my body to see that now every part of me uncovered by fabric was streaked with raw and bloody scratches.

I prepared my brain to propel my body cabin-ward. There I would reevaluate, shit, and sleep. Then I heard another cry. Only this time it wasn't a baby wail, but rather, clearly, that of an animal: guttural. I saw a glitter of light way off through thick greenery, and had the thought: That's a pool of blood if it's anything.

But by the time I'd pulled my body through that thick greenery I'd discovered that what I'd believed was a pool of blood was instead a creek. It flowed cleanly and brightly: a clarification. I should have known this by its trickle-tinkle. Yet my ears were deaf to anything but that wail. I waited for it to come again, kneeling by the edge of the water, splashing my face, my raw legs down in the suck of shore mud.

The cry came again, burred. I wondered which it was: a coyote or a mountain lion, perhaps a bear come down a bit too south for its own good. Even a feral hound, some Baskerville-by-way-of-*Deliverance* situation.

My stomach ached with imprecise fear. The beautiful green gray brown black woods showed no sign of caring. Nor did the low white sky. I was no adventurer, only a suburban girl who'd had an idea once. So I kneeled there, face dripping with creek water, waiting.

When once more the cry came I scanned the forest floor until my gaze hit it, twenty or fifteen feet down the brook. There was a small dark form heaving against bright green moss and a stand of shivering ferns. I duckwalked closer and saw it was a Hershey-colored house cat, its leg fur thickly matted with blood.

Closer I saw that the cat's wild yellow eyes were looking out into nowheresville. The channel of blood on the meat of the hip was red at the wound and darker and then syrupy where it had started to clot.

I'm no sicko, but: I wasn't used to such blood, and didn't know I'd admire it so. It was beautiful, the color and the gloss. The flies at the lab had seemed so bloodless. My own menstrual cycle was unpredictable and sloggy; that blood, full of gray-brown lumps, was nothing to admire.

The cat didn't look at me; rather, it looked insistently and blankly to the left middle distance or the upward faraway. I tasted blood in my mouth, that is how observationally empathetic I was. Or, I had been biting my lip ever since that last bullet shot, and so my teeth had loosed a plug of flesh. I remembered then the paste of the Rangoon, its sodium. From it I recalled the indignity of the group hug. I shook my head to address the present.

The cat's chest puffed out packets of air in the shade of the umbrella fern. I said aloud, "I don't want to deal with you." But I was lying. I didn't want to leave the cat to die at my hand, like this, slowly bleeding out. The bullet was plainly my fault.

And in that was a logic: the cat was now my charge. I wondered, could I kill it all the way? I couldn't. I hadn't yet done anything but stare. It's overclear that being human's not the same as being humane. But I pushed forward, trying to pretend it was.

"We've got ourselves a pet!" I hollered to Gene, but he had not followed me into the woods and so would not learn the news until later. Or would not performatively react to it until later, however that goes.

With two umbrella ferns and my shirt I made a bunting to wrap the cat. I scooped it slowly. Its needle teeth added only more injury to my beat-up arms. I took the activity as a positive sign. In the swaddling the cat rolled and rocked. I tried to hold it so it couldn't move its legs and succeeded in part as I tromped back to our cabin. I had not, it turned out, run very far afield. Presently I spotted the purple outhouse and its moon. Through the bunting I could feel the cat's heart pumping sewing machine fast. "Oh shush," I said to it, and it, tuckered and bloodied from our battle, seemed to capitulate.

What a little victory I had made, in the shadow of such a mistake. Sure, I wanted to be the one taken care of. I wanted egg noodles and swaddling. I wanted safe rest. But in absence of these things, I could be the one to take care. With not so much cost to myself. Or so I presumed at the time. I held the animal tight, warm and wet again my chest. I had to hold to mountain life. I had to forget the old, now, for here was my new, wild life, just beginning!

ONCE I GOT back in the cabin I took the tatty animal directly to the shower cube. I freed it from the shirt and ferns, then slid the door shut and waited. I pretended I could hear it breathing on the other side. I did wonder if the thing was dead.

To restore is to address violence. To violence is to disrupt a whole. I wanted to wash the cat's wound, to see what we were working with. I had never owned cat nor dog, nor bird, nor lizard, nor fish. Once Pop had asked if I wanted a dog. I think I said I didn't. Pop had already been sick. When he wasn't sick, he was "in recovery." No one ever had taught me how to respond to an animal or a bullet wound. "Gene!" I screamed. The dissolving rascal was still in absentia.

THOSE FIRST MOMENTS with that cat, my scalp pulsed hot. I wondered would I kill it or would I coddle it to health. I could not tell you what I thought then. Though now it seems ridiculous that I considered both options equally.

For soon I'd start to call the cat "the Thing." What other name might I have chosen? Leo? The Lion? The Kill? The Mouse? Sweetheart? Snooky Ookums? That last, courtesy Irving Berlin. But to each, no. This thing was a thing to me: soft, and blurred, and inexact. An announcement of presence, further details forthcoming.

I fetched the first aid kit and my needle and thread, and my lighter. I laid each of these out on the floor beside the shower cube. I got Pop's orange vial of pain pills, a bowl of water, and my least favorite T-shirt, which I ripped to strips. Needful, I congratulated myself for my quick action. I was trying to make my thoughts more orderly. I took a big breath and opened the door.

Inside the shower cube was a primetime crime scene, blood spatters and smears. I tried to catch its yellow eye like I'd find an answer—a plan, a man, a canal, Panama . . . It's easy to let oneself go in emergency, take any old scraps of hope and sew them together with your eyes closed.

Quite alive, the cat was making its demon shrills. It threw its little jaws wide. The teeth were sharp looking. It shrilled as if it thought the sound could help. As if we two were anything but victims of man and life. I dried my eyes before realizing I was midsob. "I'm doing the fucking best I can!" I told the cat but the cat didn't fucking care. In it I recognized pain.

So I jammed a crumble of pain pill into the cat's throat, feeling a tender membrane of interior cheek. Then shut the shower cube once more and waited.

After many minutes, the squall abated. I went back in, washed the lethargic animal with water, sterilized the needle with the lighter, and sewed up the wound, a deep graze which was three inches long and a quarter of an inch deep. It was like sewing a pillow: something I had done once. I found myself in shock. With antibiotic ointment I frosted the wound. Then I closed the cube once more, and took a conscious breath, exhaling wetly into the cabin, which was now otherwise quiet.

•

BETWEEN POP'S FIRST and second cancers, we went to dinner at the low-ceilinged house of a client with a five-year-old girl. Small children were then illegible to me; I didn't remember much of being small.

At first we sat on deep couches in an intact conversation pit still outfitted with shag. The father of the family offered me a ginger ale as the adults warmed their engines with respectable amounts of wine and beer. Pop was guffawing too often at things the father said, Ma nodding too much. I got embarrassed, just like a teen. Soda bubbles pin-balled in my nasal passages. I tried, with no luck, to care about what the adults were saying. The girl skipped along the edge of the gathering, a toy or doll in her hand.

After the beverages had been reduced to sloshes, the father suggested that we move to the back deck to eat and to enjoy the weather. It was late spring. We followed him through sliding doors, onto a deck with a view of their grass-and-clover quarter acre, the neighbors' trees, a bunny hutch. Pop still had twenty days on the contract. The girl asked could I sit next to her. I had no excuse but contrary desire, which I did not voice. She squirmed and smacked as I waffled. The mother asked her to sit now and to sit quietly, please. The mother herself was a quiet sitter, easy to miss. Her long hair hung to her bottom. As we began to arrange ourselves around the picnic table, Ma pulled me aside to whisper: "Denise, never trust anyone with hair that long!" When I laughed Ma said she was serious, that hair that long demonstrated a pathological lack of practicality.

While we ate palate-slicing hard-shell tacos with corn on the cob and an iceberg-and-ranch salad, it became clear that the five-year-old was growing enamored with me. For she scooped her sour cream and diced tomatoes onto my plate as little gifts. She told jokes I couldn't follow. I didn't pretend to find them funny. She pulled at my hand adhesively. Perhaps the admiration was understandable; I was a teen at the time, that last best age.

"Let's do a magic trick," she spat into my eardrum. "Can I make you disappear?" She said I should go inside and crouch behind the kitchen counter while everyone waited. I said OK, bereft of any reasonable response in the face of this sticky adorer. "Everyone!" the girl announced. "Everyone close your eyes." The adults obeyed, the rubes. I extricated myself from the picnic bench and went through the open sliding door, crouched as requested. The fridge hummed charmingly and I saw a bottle of wine close enough to grab. I thought I might just stay there for the duration of the evening, really make myself a home.

From outside I heard the grown-ups open their eyes and dramatize shock. "Where'd you put my daughter?" Pop gasped, game.

"I disappeared her!" said the kid.

"Can you bring her back?" asked her long-haired mom.

"Not yet!"

As I saw this playing out I thought it might be funny to disrupt it. I unfolded myself, crept from my retreat, and tiptoed across the linoleum. The dad and Pop were facing the kitchen, and began to open their mouths in mock surprise. Two grown men, their mouths O-made, playing this game.

"Ta-da!" I said.

The five-year-old turned and saw me and began a brawny wail. "You ruined it!" she screamed. "You ruined it!"

"It's OK," her dad said to me, as the mom went to comfort her. "We indulge her more than we should, probably." Then he announced: "We have ice cream, and cones!" The ringmaster was taking control of the crowd. The mom carried the kid inside. I no longer try to be funny in this kind of way.

Ma looked at me, smirking, and I smirked back until Pop interfered with his sad kind eyes, as if to say, it's fine now, this kind of thing, but when you're a grown-up you're going to have to learn custody for smaller, weaker things.

Too soon the mom emerged carrying the child, who was lounging on her mother's hip and licking a cone. We ate dessert. We left. On the way home I asked why they were selling. Pop said, "Oh, they're splitting up." He sold the place two weeks later, at a price no one was happy about. I'm less awful now, but it doesn't matter.

THE CAT WAS not my pet. I was its nurse. I regarded this as luck; utility need not involve the heart. Ritually, I examined the patient, built fires, argued with Gene about small domestic choices, ate soup. Gene, who'd reappeared once the yowls ceased, was upset at me for rescuing the cat. He called me a pants-wetter; he popped in and out of my days, staying just long enough to make me feel lonelier, more put-upon, once he was gone. It was now no longer summer. The cold was coming to catch us.

He strolled into the kitchen area while I was stacking dishes. "I lived, once, I think, in an apartment on Wilshire Boulevard, between the university and the cemetery, with Marjorie and a dour housekeeper who took Sundays off. She had a mole on her lip, the size and shape of a ladybug."

I let a tin plate clatter slightly. "Was she good at her job?"

"I swear sometimes I could see that thing crawl!"

"Was she good at her job?"

"I can't recall."

"That probably means she was." I wished to have said this to a real person, to have been truly valiant in this minor way, defending this woman who did or did not exist. "Did you ever have any pets?" I wanted to hear about the dogs. I couldn't remember their names.

"I don't even understand why you'd bother to ask!" He was in the front doorframe now, filling it like a villain. He did not wear a cape, but, oddly, a small Tyrolean with a feather rosy as his cheeks.

"What do you mean?"

"It doesn't matter," he said. "It doesn't matter at all. Pay attention to yourself, dearie short-pants! Time is running thin! There are beasts in the bushes! There are maggots in your meals!"

I told him to shut up. He walked out. I let go of my breath and went on with the dishes. Soon it would be time to take care of the patient once more.

FOR SEVERAL DAYS after the shooting I woke with goosebumps up my forearms, in newly cool air. I distracted myself from the cool with the cat. When it was sleeping I performed minor household duties. For instance, I decided to move the woodpile inside. I said to myself that I was worried it would snow and that the wood would get wet. Both of the wilderness handbooks seemed quite concerned about dry wood. I moved the wood from outside to inside, onto a tarp on the kitchen table, at which I had not eaten even once, despite previous desires. A degradation of these previous desires. A fun violence to domesticity. That killed an afternoon.

In order to keep the Thing sedate I fed it tri- or bi-daily crumbles of Pop's pain pills. Also I made the Thing a little bed out of towels and a blanket on the floor. The cat was like a snoozing old man, hour by hour, digesting these chemicals: It made the animal pliable and easy to wound-check. Doing so I admired its sweet soft fur, its delicate jaw-forward face. At first the skin around the stitches, crooked like bad railroad tracks, flared angry, but in a day or three settled down, with more ointment. Because of this animal I did not return to the lake. I was worried the cat would escape and die alone from its injuries. I missed swimming, already missed the hot wetness of late summer. I was aware of time and its push.

Periodically, in our early days together, the Thing yowled and I attended to it with stroking or examination or a small bowl of the rice mush I had been feeding it. I recalled, over and over, how "the Thing" was not really a name.

Every time Gene showed up, he showed up complaining. With a drippy, honking nose. With eye-bags big enough to travel the world. With suspicious lesions at his thinning hairline. As the Thing strengthened, he was worsening. I do not mean to make a causality here. But to describe a coincidental

parallel which, like a North and South Pole, pinned me spin-
ning. "Marjorie?" he'd bellow from the back room.

"Wrong number!" I'd respond.

On the mountain it became clear to me that I had no obvious
art. Of course my talents were compulsion and self-haunting.
And Gene was the result. What pride could I take in that. So
instead I stroked the cat's bony head. I curled up. I lived.

AT FIRST IT was just relentless percussion: roof-tap and timpani.
This was what rain in the woods was like. I witnessed it from
inside the only building in view. In the suburbs heavy rain had
always made me irritable, though a little drizzle never provoked
anything. In college for my science requirement I had taken a
course on hydrology and water management thinking it would
soothe me, to know how each liquid molecule dispersed to gas
and then reconstituted toward earth. Instead the course was a
drag, packed with students majoring in landscape management.
They would go on to work at golf courses and parks.

The rain, steady, beat through the morning. I got up from
the back bottom bunk, where I'd been attempting sleep for at
least five hours. I had not slept well since shooting the cat. Nor
did I feel I deserved to.

When I rose I saw the Thing had drug itself from its towel-
blanket nest. Now it lay where the wood and the linoleum met.
The wisp-thin molding bisected its dark pity. "Oh, Thingy," I
said. "Oh, cat!" And stooped to give little Thing a pat, which it
curled into. It was indeed a pleasingly wild thing, by turns vacant and mean or weak and demure. That is a romantic affect.

For, simply: sometimes the cat came to me. Other times it did not have the will to fight. Presently I scooped its little heft into my arms. A dingle of shit fell from its bottom to the floor. The rain was now quieting, faucet dripping. I bounced the cat like a babe as I ventured forward, to open the front door, to stand on the porch and watch the rain evaporate into a downy mist.

I stood on the porch with the Thing, and told it: "Here is our world as it looks now, as we should always remember it." What a sap. All around the mist laid itself on the blunt and sharp and curved landscape, robing the trees and grasses and brambles and stones in a thin and glittering film.

The cat let out a loose bellow, pushing its paws into my lower abdomen. It was the strangest thing—I had discovered— that the cat had no claws at all. Though this made me less tentative, handling it, I did wonder: how it had survived alone? A bird cawed and shot out against the tree line. The day was warmer but not hot. The cat dug its forelegs into the softest part of my stomach, the organs. "Simmer," I said to it. "Hush." Everywhere the earth was rain softened, steam hissing from loam. I may have imagined this.

Just then a tree of lightning cracked out in the distance, on the horizon, out past our valley and beyond the nearest summit. A roil of thunder then cupped the peak, causing the cat to stir rigid before settling. Then the Thing began to purr, the baby.

I had become comfortable caring for this cat. It was a blend of obligation and generosity: a human submission. The wound was by this time healing slowly around the stitches, pinkly and with a shine. The cat ranged into the yard sometimes, but more often stuck by me.

Now I resigned to the couch and its soft wiles. I was so tired. The Thing approached to lay beside me, waggling its butt like a drunk. Its smell was honeyed and dank, not unlike the smell of the lab flies' sweet-rot fare, that hanging labor odor. Outside it began to rain again and went on raining. It would go on for many days.

ONE DAY IN the rain Gene showed up on the doorstep, holding a fistful of dripping black-eyed Susans. "What are you supposed to be?" I asked him, snorting the humid dirt smell of the woods.

"A gentleman caller," he said, while chewing on his bottom lip. His left eye was twitching enough to warrant an exam. I stepped up close to him, looked at him in his big dirty pores. "You can come in," I said. "But we're not talking about the weather."

"So you say, little lady!" he exclaimed, and showboated in, tracking or not tracking mud.

I stayed unspeaking, would only look at the cat: my new confidante. Eventually he left, miffed. I am happily left, I thought. Or, as Garbo said—not as herself but as a spent ballerina in *The Grand Hotel* (1932)—"I want to be alone . . . I just want to be alone." The amplified repeat was my favorite part. I didn't need my old things anymore. I didn't need anything, really. The cat was okay company. The cat didn't talk.

We stayed dry together. For generally I preferred to stay either dry or completely saturated. Because of this preference I did not leave the cabin. To pee I had taken to straddling the shower cube, then washing it down with a cold hoseful of water. To shit—which was less often, as I had reduced my calories and fiber dramatically, out of convenience—I did slop through the mud to the purple outhouse with its moon door. There I sat in that gross little prism and opened up my backhole.

Something about the mountain air and rain made me feel loose, celebratory, despite my persistent lostness. I congratulated myself for having had the foresight to move the firewood. But it was not enough to keep my mood buoyed. For it would not stop raining, water washing the days in and out in a tireless pulse. A week of this weather.

Sometimes in this close lull I'd catch myself thinking of my loved ones, the audience to my disappearing act, and get a rising acid wave up my throat. I'd pet the cat and breathe. Unbidden, a photo or painting of something I'd never seen: Pop, Ma, and Ken, sitting calmly at a dinner table. I did not think they'd be better off without me. My leaving had no selflessness in it. Even the scant absence I had by then wrought—unexplained, but explicable—had given me a thrill. If I was not happy on the mountain, I was not unhappy either.

In the deep of night, lightning began to crack more aggressively, all over the valley. I woke and stood on the porch with the Thing in my arms and we watched it. The lightning came charging through the small hatches where the trees opened up to the sky. I was an animal in shelter, holding another animal, which I had hurt, but which was healing. I was tired, listening to thunder, seeing the lightning, counting between them. Rolling onto the floor I watched to see if the cat stirred with any thunder clap. One Mississippi, two, three, four, five. Clap. The cat did not. I then returned to the bottom of the bunk to sleep, a dupe for nature's next blow.

I WOKE THINKING: earthquake, tornado, hurricane. There was a mean wet wind lashing itself across my everything. Despite this I kept my eyes closed for a good few minutes. As soon as I opened them, I would have to deal with whatever this was.

I counted again, once more in Mississippi's. When I got to one hundred, I opened my eyes. There was water on my face.

It is raining in the cabin, was my first coherent thought. My eyes opened.

Is this an end, I thought. Am I dying.

No, for it is wet. Unless death is wet.

My logic was a dial tone, dulled further by the blood-thrum in my ears. My eyes were not feeding my head logical data. I yelled into the cold wet wind: "Fuck!" And that seemed to calm everything for one moment.

My shivering body was still under blankets but it was also under dead leaves and branches. A few were mere inches from my face, poking and bladed. I perceived my luck, unpoked, before I perceived the size of the situation. I think more often it is the other way around.

At last I allowed myself to think the thought: a tree has fallen through the roof.

Or, a large section of tree has fallen through a large section of roof.

I felt the scrambling of my perception, as when I had

awakened that morning at Omar's. Had that only been a month prior. Two. I visualized a calendar. I began to count the days, then stopped. I cleared this away. Reapproached.

Let it be known: I did not think about death very much, when once a tree nearly fell on top of me. I had been sleeping in a cabin in a remote mountain valley. I had a common impulse of survival. If I may be congratulated for any old achievement, let it be that.

Then another piece of roof heaved in and the shock was over.

Where is my biggest tarp, I wanted to know. I remembered. My biggest tarp was underneath the wood on the kitchen table. The wind was trammeling the valley. It had knocked the tree down. I shielded myself with my covers, my sleeping bag, a deep breath, before deciding what to do.

Plan: nail the blankets up between the rooms. Free up the tarp. Nail that up too. Start a fire. Forget the bedroom. Go the long way around the cabin to the latrine once outdoors is possible again. Practice partially ignorant living, regarding: tree in cabin, regarding: roof open to elements.

Gathered myself and lumbered upward, out of the bed. Used the tree branch as a counterbalance: launched myself out into the sodden bedroom where all corners had gone soft. A branch made a thwack as I landed on the wet wood. More roof crumbled from the edge of the hole, black and glossy. Stepped forward slowly as if on ice. Took me a minute to get to the stove or five. Was gasping, possibly in fright. Shoveled the burnt stuff out into the bucket. Retrieved split logs thankfully adjacent on kitchen table.

Gathered semi-dry tinder from a corner of the room. Stuffed it meaningfully into the metal belly. Tried to light a match. Where was my lighter. Tried to light another match. Blown out; blown out, by powers more forceful than my own little lungs. At last, hunched, got the wood aflame. I turned to extract the tarp.

When I turned back, to check on the little fire: smoke. The metal chimney had been bent and crushed into a series of breakneck crimps. The outside clean metal, the inside tarred. Fine black dust everywhere, a powdery explosion. I tried to get water, but no water came from the faucet. Didn't use all of my jugs of drinking water to stop it: I wasn't dumb, just shocked. I took only the littlest jug, and dumped it. The fire hissed as if to attack. Then it submitted, saying goodbye in a doublewide white-smoke bonanza. Held my sleeve in front of my mouth, then, I think, blacked out.

When I came to, shock freshened, I surged.

Once all the wood was on the floor I seized the freed tarp. Scaled the bed with nails and the axe. Coughed and hammered the nails with the butt of those tall rafters, bones clattering against each other. Clothes damp on the inside, damper on the out. Everything was miserable. I mean: I was miserable. Here I couldn't live, couldn't be dry. The wind bulged the tarp. I might as well've been nude and dipped in honey, defenseless and licked.

Remembered then the tower I had seen on the horizon. Thought I knew in what direction it stood. Held on to this cadged certainty. Began to prep. Turned on the lantern and began to disembowel the tubs. Not neatly. Found what I needed:

bars, ropes, necessities only, the knives, dry goods. Dry, what a joke. Filled the emptied plastic tub with these and then with water jugs and some other heavy things to drag along. Trussed the tub with a length of cord. Could I be a sled dog, running through the wilds with my sled in tow. Where was I going again.

Undressed myself in the cold damp. Dressed myself in all the clothes I could find, including Earl John's overalls. I was in a panic. Put on my boots. Tied them in bald knots. Could not find the wilderness guidebooks. Looked for them, distressed, for a minute. But a compass: I had that, and I took it out with me, and my haphazard tub kit, all into the bolting storm.

By the time I was in the real outdoors my heavy boots sucked into shit-brown mud. Was it my imagination, how I could feel the mud turning to ice water at my ankles, where the overall cuffs were loose and sopping? I felt my legs and feet acutely: the muscles torqueing themselves into great hard ropes—how when I dug my toes into a mud clot, a sensation of work ran itself up to my butt. My shoulders went asymmetrical with dragging.

When the torrent stopped suddenly, I thought of doubling back. How long had it been since I left, how far? Then I remembered the ruin of the cabin. There was no place for me there. I required operable shelter.

The sun was now entirely up. The journey to the tower felt unstoppable. Though every so often my body stopped, to lean against a tree, to survey the motionless woods, while my muscles fizzed. I saw nothing except my own misfortune. Yes my footprints in the mud were lonely. The cat was not with me. I doubled over, sweat. My heaving dumb mortality, my sexless exertion. I walked along a strange river. I checked my compass, wiped its face of condensation. On the horizon I could see the tower, and I ran, clumsily, forward. A new cloud slung itself over me. It began to rain again.

UP CLOSE I found the tower rusty. In another circumstance it would have been beautiful, standing there like a valiant ruin in a wide plot of ornate weeds. I got under. Beneath its shelter, there in the mud I stood heaving, then sat on the plastic bin to think. The structure was maybe forty feet tall, with three bands of crossbars evenly spaced, each with a thin perimeter of walkway. Between each crossbar, the height of two tall humans. Between the final crossbars and the shelter, there was a ladder. It looked as if there'd once been ladders, too, between the lower measures, but they'd since been removed, metal sawed away. There were snubs of rungs where perhaps my boots would find purchase, or so I hoped. I would need to be able to get myself up each lower section of the tower.

Each time I untucked my chin to survey the tower above, the gusting sideways rain threatened to drown me. My lip cracked where I had bitten it. The blood was briefly warm, then not. There was no trace of movement but the weather and its beating of the mountain and the valley. I would not be able to bring everything I had brought with me, up. So I packed some of the water, food, and sundries in a flannel and tied it like a rucksack to my back. The wind sounded like a river. My heart sounded like a heart, amplified. It was night. It was still night, or night again, or dark morning. And while it was still dark I made myself stand beneath the tower and drink water and not die. I walked in tight circles.

I made yet another plan: how to get up. I would use my ropes. I would scrabble up the tower, then simply wait there in secure shelter until the rain stopped. I would be high and impervious to flooding. For now beneath the tower I felt safer. Its structure divided the wind's momentum and spitting grit. Here, I squatted.

For some time, I tried to remember how to tie a figure-eight knot, which is something I had learned the single summer I'd been sent away to camp, the summer after Pop's first sick note. It had been a Jewish sleepaway camp, on a mountain campus populated with plank-cabins and a lake, a dining hall. A taciturn, nonpracticing halfling, I had mostly been ignored. As a result I had learned nothing social, no lessons of friendship. There in the woods and meadows not even a crush crept.

However at this camp were some short cliffs where, three times a week, a red-cheeked Australian taught us to climb with ropes and harnesses. I had thrown myself into this, up these cliffs, and down them—belay on, and so forth. It had been the most successful element of summer. Though in the intervening time I had not thought of ropes, nor harnesses.

Now with pleasurable effort I remembered the Australian's face. I tried to remember his mouth and the words which had been formed there. I had ropes, and a need to use them. I thought: You have a head for things like this. But in fact I did not.

This new climb ahead, I worked to perform my old camp vigor. I began to play with a length of cord. By and by I made a knot that looked right enough: a two-headed loop-de-snake. Then I undid it, and snatched out my hummingbird knife, with its carabiner end, and knotted it to the end of the cord and threw it wildly over the first crossbar. It hit the crossbar, which thrummed percussive.

I knotted again a provisional figure eight, put my boot down and stepped, then hovered there six inches in air for a sick moment. At last I began. I worked upward slowly, holding on to the cord knot for balance. It was not a steady climb, but with the help of the rung snubs, I moved intermittently upward with tortoise confidence. My biceps hollered as I did.

It was not until I was on the second tier, in the dead middle of the climb, that I remembered I'd lost track of the Thing. This was a new smolder in the ashes of my empathy. The cat would die or not die. My lungs worked like a bellows. I clung to the pole until they slowed. I was, of course by this time, an expert at flicking guilt away into unexplored corners. It was only the realization—come so late—that I'd lost the Thing, which shocked me then. Water dripped into my eye. I squinted until it flushed down my cheek. A serviceable cry for a serviceable animal, now gone. My clothing was saturated, my palms torn to shreds. Yet here I needed only rise.

And rise I did, feeling the ad hoc rucksack try to pull me back to earth with its heft, over and over. My boots slipped on the nubbins of the sawn-off rungs. I ripped an overall pant leg, revealing the damp thermal underwear beneath. I wiped my face and tasted blood. I was bleeding into the world. The clouds were hemorrhaging still.

When I got to the highest, final set of crossbars, I allowed myself to look down. There my plastic tub was a dark mirror, already filled with water. Too, the mud ruts marking where I'd paced were brimming. It was not until I'd gotten to the top of the ladder that I tried to look outward and around, across the land. For a moment in my sorry state I was sure I could smell things that weren't there: musk, citrus, orange blossom. My body working to calm me down, pulling all the wrong stops.

There was the lake; there were mountain peaks and weeping woods; there was a wet bigness all around me—me, the smallest of motes. I had climbed. In the corner was a silhouette, a shadowed big body boy. Oh, Gene. Oh, sorry me! Escaped from an escape only to find this vintage ogre. I worked to catch my breath. I sat. I counted down from one hundred as if I were alone. And then slept long as I needed.

WHEN I WOKE it was still raining and someone was blowing in my face. I grunted like an animal. It was only Gene, with his sparkler eyes. "Huzzah!" he said. In some berserker mood he whipped and galloped from one end of the rickety room to the other.

"Who's that?" I said: I wanted to lob a blow.

"Huzzah! Huzzah! Huzzah!" he bellowed. "It is I!"

"Oh you," I said. "Of course," I said.

Once my eyes were open all the way Gene straightened and began to stride about the room, a gentleman down the boulevard. His mood, these days, was mutable as the weather. "You reckon we'll be flooded out?"

"No," I said. "The rain should stop eventually." I began to strip my layers, one by one, wringing out each article, and draping them across the wood floor.

"Lady!" Gene said. "Please!"

"As if you haven't seen this." I continued the most disappointing burlesque this side of any river.

"We must have our delicacies!" he said. "We must have some assurances between creature and man!"

"I'm an animal, same as you, Geney," I said. "In fact you're not even—"

"And what of the real animal?"

"The real—"

"The kitty?"

"Gone," I said sternly, now down to my skivvies. I laid my gear to dry across the floor. "Drop it."

"Seems to me—" he began.

"Drop it," I said, and, ignoring him, began to inventory my injuries. First, there were my hands, the messes: flesh shreds, and rutted rope burns across my palms. The old scratches broken open, pinkly. The new notch on my shin, purpling. Blisters on my heels, ankles, and toes; some burst into raw newborn craters. The split in the lip and its sexual swelling. A septum raw from sniveling. Never before had I been so busted. It was exhilarating to be a dumb body, unhealed.

Next I took stock of my surrounds. The room was a cube, with a flat roof, and two windows in each wall. Each window was cheerily mullioned into quarters. The glass was long gone, and though the wind and rain cut through the openings, it did not drown me. The plank wood floor was warped with age into liquid lines and gaps showcasing the mud ground four stories below. Looking down I felt vertigo, as if my chest were being slightly dislocated from my throat. In this dislocation, a feverish flash: I remembered standing in Omar's living room. I had been this high before. Perhaps this was just another place to crest before a plummet.

I resolved to stop looking down. Quickly my vertigo thawed into a cleaner awareness. I looked at the room. It was almost empty. On one wall, an old torn map with a rusty pin near its center, which seemed to connote the location of the tower. The land north, east, south, west was wrinkled with water lines, with humps and peaks. I wasn't interested in where I was however. Except that I saw I had traveled to the edge of the park.

The notion came like sleet. How surprised I was to be within a formalized territory. My solitude had been undone. This smarted. Then, tasting bile, I leant out the doorway and vomited into the space below. My digestive tract was a two-way street. Over and over, the acid, the silvery tang. I scraped my tongue with my fingernails to find relief.

"Take it easy, you wild young thing," Geney said, standing beside me. I looked away from him and closed my eyes, feeling a plummeting inside my innards—or in an emotional concept of my innards, which felt endless.

"Hey," he croaked. "Tell me."

"Tell me what?" I slurred with woe.

"Who eats floating fish but flies?"

"Who eats floating fish but flies?"

"Who eats floating fish but flies?"

"Turn it off, you sentimental jerk," I said, pressing down on an extra bad blister. The pressure issued sentries of focusing pain. I could not say then why it caused me so much harm, hearing him ape and reference the life we had left. However I recognized in this, in him, a repurchased coherence. I wondered what had changed.

"You wouldn't be half-bad if you acted like a woman once in a blue moon."

I sniveled and glared. "It hasn't ever mattered whether I'm one way or another to you, has it?"

"Only in regard to social niceties, Denise. Only in that regard."

The rain went on hammering the tower. I wondered, in a self-dramatizing way, if I would ever again stand on solid ground. I looked out, not down, and my chest surprised me: It yowled wild for the cat. The range was struck by the shadows of long clouds, their fleet travel. Gene was rapping a tune on the doorway, looking out on the land: pad-a-whack, tap-tap, pad-a-whack. Then he began to laugh: huh-huh, huh-huh-huh. "I don't see why you bother with that little nothing. That pipsqueak. That bear snack."

I looked back at him, squinted, spit, peeled off a hunk from an energy bar. "What are you talking about?"

"The cat."

"You loved your dogs so much you slept in the same bed as them."

"Animals are animals and men are men."

"Go on," I said, looking beyond at the clouds blurring themselves on distant peaks.

"Denise, I gotta say something." He didn't look blue but he did look serious.

"What?"

"When I got sick and sad and had to leave the lodge for good—"

"Was that when you died, after you had to leave?"

"—the dogs didn't come with me."

"You don't have to tell me about that."

"About which?"

"You choose." He didn't answer. "The dogs," I cued. "They couldn't very well fit in your apartment on Wilshire. Marjorie wouldn't have liked that."

He took a pause, then said: "There were too many to shoot them in their sleep." How could I have been surprised. I did not say a thing. "One woulda got up and started barking and then the others, and well—let's say it wouldn't'a been elegant."

"Did you poison them?" I was trying to see how I felt regarding this. Could I be sentimental about dogs that had never lived? Sure. I accepted that clawless Thingy had punctured something: me. It was I who'd sprung a leak.

"I put brandy in their slop. Waited for them to get drunk and bendy. Guess I could have poisoned them but it didn't seem heroic."

"You've gotta be heroic."

"Sure," he said, seeming not to catch my near-dead deadpan.

"I think as a kindness I meant to shoot Lucie first. As you recall she was my favorite. Except when I got the rifle out, this crazy stud, this setter mix, got excited cause he thought we were going hunting. He was one of the bigger ones and I guess maybe he didn't get as soused as the others, who were wobbling out back in the yard. But he started to bound toward me, Denise, and I let the rifle go off, shot him square in the brain. Small mercy," he laughed. "Small, small mercy."

I got off my duff and began to approach him. The floor announced me, keening.

"Once I got the first cap off I shot them quick as I could. Bap-bap-bap," he explained. "Course Lucie looked at me, the small, wet-eyed little bitch, and I shot her too. You should have seen the yard. Some died quickly. Miserable stuff. Others I had to kick their heads in." Gene was sweating and I saw this as I moved closer.

I am a woman of average height, and he a man of average height, so when I got very close to him my eyes were aligned with a deep parabolic fold in his thick neck. There the skin was pink with a sallow undertone, and visibly damp.

"They were just mutts, Denny. Just animals," he said, in that dissolving gravel voice of his. "Just goddamn dogs."

I've heard people say they can't stand a sad animal story. I can. But this was something about decency. I set both palms on his sodden leviathan chest, pushed.

Wrestling is the natural way of fighting in this county—as boxing is too quick and requires much thinking and concentration.

CARSON McCULLERS,
The Ballad of the Sad Café

When I pushed Gene from the tower it was not an exorcism. Nor was it heroic. I watched him plummet but he was gone before the ground, evaporated up. Later that day the rain stopped. I did not and do not connect the two.

I gathered up my things. I dressed, in a shirt and overalls and boots, all only slightly dank. I wasn't sad. What I was, in this new absence, was finally alone. By the time I was ready to descend the tower the rain had started up, again, harder.

So I waited. In a tantrum of boredom I threw my carbon steel blade into a post beam and it stuck there. It may be there still. I had a whole angry standoff with the hole I'd ripped in Earl John's overalls. The sucker had nothing to say. Soon, shiftless, I fantasized that on the plank floor sat a bowl of gleaming oranges. I wanted to eat one like an apple, sink my teeth through the oily peel and bitter pith, down into the popping pulp. Did I wonder if Gene would come back? At the time I assumed he would. I didn't spend time or hurt on it, not then. Rather I dedicated my heart to the cat. Though I assumed it was dead, or halfway to Tipperary.

The rain stopped, started again, poured then drooled then spat. At last it stopped and seemed to stay stopped. I waited to see if it would start again. I waited half a day, then through the night, wondering if another storm would roll in. By and by—as I watched the light once more surge into the crevices of the valley—I began to think about how I would fix the cabin. Whether I could find some way to call Earl John. I recognized: I had an unwillingness to call Earl John. I had an inability to fix the roof. But I would return to the cabin and figure things out from there.

Perhaps my first plan was the best: I would return and set about securing the tarp—and perhaps some blankets and other things as insulation—against the cabin's gash. Then I would return to swimming, return to my ecstatic ignorant lonesomeness. When it got even cooler I would cease swimming and search for peace inside, I mean, indoors. Perhaps at last I'd learn how to tie those knots properly, should the need again arise. Then I could expire as scheduled, in some new future quiet.

Softly I remembered the push of my hands through air. In the end Gene was the Lucie and I was not.

It was dawn and then sunrise and then day: the sky stayed a markless blue. In this day I was not anything to anyone but myself. Only briefly did I reflect on the desire for faith: prayer beads, powders, herbs, a god. I had felt this want in clawing flashes. I am not a person of faith. I believe only in fumbling cause, only in stinging effort.

Now I was myself only. The boards of the tower whined low. I looked out across the mantis-colored weeds and the darker thicket of bushes and the trees in their enflamed autumnal state, and the far peaks' angles cutting up the smooth line of clouds, when, in the spreading daylight, something down below the tower moved. There a fleet shadow darted. A heat flushed through.

At first it was merely a moving shadow; it could have been anything. But as the sun rose the vision was revealed. Wouldn't you know it was that cat, making a last-act hullo. It seemed to me a possibility, and therefore, in my state, a probability.

Without knowing what I was doing I all but tumbled down the tower. No decision or resolve necessary. In the rush I was lucky to remember to scoop up my hummingbird knife and my compass. Leave the jug and the eats to the birds, I thought, descending. My carbon steel blade in the beam, forget it. I had a cat to catch.

As I wrenched downward I could tell something indecent was happening in my shoulder and trunk. My body revealed a thin, deep ache with each utter of descent. No rope, no net. I shimmied like a bear. The metal caught me when it could, but its effects were just minor entries into my body's sorry tabulations.

The earth when I met it was mud. At last, I was down. After how many days? Could've been that I'd a broken rib. My medical knowledge was dodgy, limited to cancer-patient relief. I was therefore happy to be back on the ground. However the switching shadow was now not anywhere. I kicked the plastic tub. Its water trembled. I left it where it was, a dull monument to a couple of desperate days. I was doing the best I could.

That's a lie, but: I let the ground support me. By this I mean I sunk into the mud, butt first, and crossed my legs onto themselves. The mud was cold but there was a bottom to it, so I sat, secure, and reminded my lungs to march in line. I closed my eyes and pretended I was preparing to die. Then I got up, because I was no one to anyone but myself. I could not stop thinking this.

I WALKED FOR quite some time. I can't say how long. My use of the compass was bungling: I stumbled one way, and then another, until by some dumb magic I ended up at a wide, deep lake in a valley. It was not any lake. It was mine, swollen with rainwater. All its marginal greenery was tamped down and washed sideways. I skirted the shore until I came to the blonde meadow.

There were large birds surfing the sky overhead as I made my way across it. There were red-winged blackbirds, slight and darting, flashing their hot markings outward. My steps made crunching and sucking sounds alternately. I was either breaking through mud crust or wading through vegetal sludge.

Every tree was a duplication of the next. I am not a naturalist; I'd wanted only to leave. In doing so I hadn't suddenly become a Goodall, an Audubon, a whomever. So even after everything— the up-the-tower and the down-the-tower—this wilderness walking was just an unremarkable commute. There was a greenish vestibule, a gray and gray and brown vestibule. I moved through this landscape like a mall-walker in poor condition.

Though I was not entirely resistant to nature. I heard a bit of a crash and a significant movement of grasses. "Hello?" I said. Because you can take the fool out of the suburbs but you can't take the fool out of her.

And then! The grasses drew back to accommodate my friend, brown and matted and skinny and indigent, moving like a trusty river towards me: the Thing. "Hello," I said again and quickly scooped it up. In my arms it wound itself into a dumpling, a donut shape, and then was stretching, ferrety. It pawed at me in greeting, and went on scrabbling. For a moment I thought, is this indeed Thingy? It was. Or it was as good as— no. It was. Its eyes were warm lime gems; I grinned terribly into the buggy wild light. I did not wonder where the cat had been, was not compassionate or curious in this regard. I registered only the cat's return.

I was once more something to something. It felt okay. I sat to make a lap. Then, unbuttoning my shirt from beneath the overalls I removed it and then fashioned it into a sling for the Thing, as I had when I had injured and then rescued it. I lifted up the darling, struggling to get vertical, hurting a bit. Around the furry body I resecured the overall bib. The cat slapped its paw around my wrist like a bracelet. I was now topless except for the bib and my cat, but who was my modesty for? I was an animal with an animal, anonymous, homeward. I had pushed through to a new kind of nakedness. Or so I believed. I was not a person, anymore, who need close any door behind me.

I pressed my face downward against the soft tickle of cat fur. I blushed with quick joy and said, "Welcome to our new lives!"

On we went, walking in one direction, waking to our new days. As we moved my nipples snagged the breeze. Otherwise I was not thinking about nakedness, or what nakedness had

formerly meant. I was thinking about how I might intuit myself into a knowledge of carpentry. How perhaps I could fix the
roof. Of course I would not go and try to find people or a phone.
I accepted to myself that I was feral now, that in escaping I had
made a choice that would chart my future days and death.

While walking I did idly wonder what animals I would
find in the cabin, what disarray. It would be good, I thought, to
confront the entropy. To embrace a surprise, to discover, to not
know till.

I could live among the animals I would find there: the deer
whose tracks I'd never seen, nestling with bears behaving be-
nevolently as sofas and recliners; foxes and mice mincing along
the woodpile, spiders weaving in the corners impressive silver
warps and wefts; did the foxes go after the mice; yes; did the
mammals note the weavers; they did; were the fawns wary of
the bears; they were; and there was the Thing; yes; the cat, safe
and purring demurely, tail tapping lightly on a molding, or in
the folds of the bedclothes, snoozing, batting its paws on the
bark of the fallen tree above, snoozing more, snoozing in peace,
snoozing in satisfaction and satiety. How pretty my brain had
become. It made me want to spit.

Moving through the meadow I started to feel a great relief,
convinced that I would find a way to fix the roof or to live beneath its rupture. I thought about whistling. I didn't whistle.

The cabin came into view. From my vantage, through
pines, it looked just as I had left it. The front porch was clear of
branches, creatures. My teeth were grinding but I did not register this as a sign. I found that holding my arm kept my shoulder

from aching so I held the meat of my bicep, pressing it close to my sternum, the kitten along with it.

As we moved closer to the cabin, I saw movement through the trees. I had my pet safe in one arm and snatched my hummingbird knife into the other. I advanced like this. I took care not to break branches underfoot. I crouched behind a high wall of brambles. There was a man dragging a large branch with dead leaves attached, across the cabin's dirt yard. He was tall and thin and wore a long-sleeved shirt and a pair of ripped jeans. His hair was curly and hung to his chin—thick, a dormouse color—and his eyes were set far apart, koi-like. His limbs gangled, or, they hung there, dragged by his long thin trunk. He was some woodsy methed-out young Jagger, with a misplaced, unuseful cool. For no reason I thought of the man on the train, how he hadn't moved to give up his seat. The trespasses felt somehow twinned; inside me the same blaze raged.

I did not immediately say hello, nor did I approach. Rather I watched this lean, ugly man invade my little yard, dragging more and more branches and stacking them in a pile. Then I watched as he knocked his boots on the edge of the porch steps and went in my cabin like he owned the place. Only once he was gone from sight did I belatedly jump. This startled the cat, who bit into the softest part of my chest and so I yelped in pain— loud and high enough to peel the bark off every goddamn tree. I held fast to the cat despite this, though it bucked and squirmed.

I trapped my breath in the chamber of my throat. It pressed against my lips. I waited to see if the man would emerge from the cabin, to investigate the noise. I patted the Thing to see if it would calm, and it did. I watched it nuzzle as my body hummed with sudden fear, with the knowledge of my situation: a young woman about to be confronted by a strange man.

Could he be a reasonable person.

Could I go up there and say to him: Hello, this is the cabin I have rented from an older man who seems a little disappointed in life but generally happy, who gave me these very overalls as a gesture of care and custody.

Could I offer to share the cabin.

Could we two rattle around this small corner of this big world, never subscribing to any messy emotional attachments, never looking for a high, never broaching a low—

I began to imagine a hammock of a life, with this lanky companion.

Then, I thought: Stop! Stop charming yourself out of the seriousness of the situation.

He was an invader, plain. A burglar-vagabond-usurper. And here I was now, charged with the task of recapturing my haunt.

I closed my eyes a moment to gather myself. To gather and then surge.

When I opened them, the man was square in front of me, pointing a pistol at my chest. Fumbling, I extended my knife's blade into the light, a dancer holding her hand to waltz. The Thing shifted its weight and then through some wriggle managed to jump away. Momentarily the man followed the motion of the cat with the gun. "No!" I squealed.

This was the first pitiful syllable I'd said to any human in some time. For even then I was not so deluded to think that Gene might count as a conversation partner. I was just a shoe-string escapist, weak from my travails, out of practice and alone. And this stranger was an invader on my little isle of non-man.

I stood up like a bully because what was there to do. Though doing this I was aware of my tits, flagrante. I did not celebrate this but rather bore the fact, then said with more self-surety: "That's my house. And that looks a lot like my gun."

"You some kind of yeti?" he joked, leering loosely. "Some kind of mountain man?"

"Is that my gun?" I asked.

"You leave your gun on the ground back in the woods?" he asked. His words slipped from his slash mouth. He looked as forgotten as I hoped to be.

Had it been, then, a week, or two, since I had heard the baby wailing, the baby that had been in the end poor Thingy? Longer? I felt a vertiginous slosh, as I had in the tower, as I had at Omar's. I was always higher and lower than I wanted to be, then. Spare me the finer points of wanting to live on a moun-tain. I did it anyway. "Maybe."

"Then, yeah. This is probably your gun."

But looking at him, I saw the gun had found a more right-ful owner. The way he held it now at his sharp hip, with confi-dence. His stance was something from a film; I wondered had he learned it somewhere. I wanted the gun back, but knew I couldn't ask. "My mother has a shop down-mountain, sells pieces like these."

"That outfitter?"

"That's my mother you bought it from, then."

"Skinny, like you."

"Yeah I guess."

"Your mother was specific about its handling."

"My own father died at a shooting range, is why she's like that," Haw said. "Shot himself through the teeth with a .45, which his buddies cleaned up."

Of course I didn't believe him. Would anyone? I tried to imagine a man romantic and mad enough to off himself that way, a son who would so eagerly disclose. I couldn't. "But she still sells guns?"

"Wasn't the gun's fault."

"What are we going to do?"

He looked at me like I was a banana peeling itself. "What do you mean?"

"I'm just wondering what you're doing here," I said, straightening myself up. The Thing was on the porch now, stalking back and forth, as if nothing was different. What cruelty.

"I come up here sometimes," he said, putting his gun-free hand up in the air.

"But I'm here now. I rented this place. Paid money."

"Let's get you cleaned up," he said, and put his narrow back to me, sauntering toward the porch and the cat.

I freed my boot from the brambles and followed him in. Let myself take big breaths as I climbed the stairs.

Once inside, I looked around and saw all of my possessions rearranged. The kitchen table was neat, chairs orderly, and the firewood that had been thrown to the floor was nowhere to be

seen. The sun-shaped trivet had been replaced upon the table,
I noted. It was not any anarchy, what had befallen here. There
was a small heap of clothes and blankets in the corner of the
front room. I nodded at it. "My name is Haw," the man told me.
Then I told him my name though I wished I hadn't.

"Sit down, Denny," he said, walking to the table in the front
room. I didn't, though I was exhausted. I had to make a demon-
stration. Sure: a stand. It was in these moments that I was feeling the vagaries of the whole foolhardy, outdoorsy spiel. Not
when I shot the cat. Not when the tree fell. Not when I lost the
cat. But now, with this man here, spoiling the view.

Seeing I was to remain standing, Haw began to give me
a brief tour of his alterations. For in all of his homeliness and
stray-cat manners, he was yet that kind of man. "See, I fixed
the roof," he said. "So, you're welcome for that." I saw that I was
supposed to be grateful. I did not make any particular expression. Inside I steamed.

Across the hole there were rough split logs nailed and making a serviceable patch. I saw that the hole was in fact not so
large, perhaps three feet in diameter.

"Uh," I said at last. "Oh," I said. I felt unreal, half-naked,
conversing with this stranger. I did not feel like myself at all.

"And the stove, see?"

I looked over to see the pipe all hammered out, a flame inside. "I do." The fire felt accusatory. The cabin was no longer on
my terms exclusively.

"I reset the pump, too. This place was a mess when I got
here." He crossed his arms over his chest loosely.

In gestural response I pulled at the bib of my overalls. "Yeah?" I did not feel comfortable but discomfort was hardly the worst thing I had recently experienced.

"Where have you been, anyway?" he asked.

I thought for a moment. "I was out in a tower a few miles out, an old lookout or something."

"You were out there through that whole storm going across the range?"

"Yep."

"How'd you even get up there?"

"Climbed."

"Climbed! No wonder you're so banged up." He had the nerve to laugh so I laughed along with him—the old school trick of laughing-with. It was mania. "You'd think a girl could climb up the tower could maybe just stay and fix that roof."

"What can I say," I said flat.

"It was tricky to fix that roof but I split some of that wood you had and covered it. For EJ's sake. The stuff that wasn't green at least. It'll do for now."

So he knew Earl John. I felt like I was supposed to be impressed. He walked around the perimeter, preening, looking at me from angles only.

I shrugged. "Did you call Earl John already? I've got his number." Indeed it was there in my memory still, summoned by cue.

"You think there's phone reception out here?"

I shrugged again.

"I'll let him know when I get back down-mountain."

"When's that gonna be?"

"You that eager to get rid of me?"

I walked over to the bracing beam and examined it, tested it. "Seems a little wiggly."

"Wiggly my ass." He ape-smiled. "Wonder if you'll help me finish up on the roof? There's actually a little leak I was noticing."

I nodded. "Can you give me a sec to rest?"

"Sure can. Sure can."

Then like a host he got us both water. We sat down across from one another at that kitchen table. Once I had wanted just this, this sitting, though solo. We drank the water and looked at each other. It was the most domestic I'd felt in these weeks on the mountain. He laughed a little unhinged laugh and I saw that his teeth were bad. There was a missing one. A front tooth half-gray. And along the bottom, up front, they overlapped as if in a huddle. I did not put a value on this. It merely filled out the portrait.

"We alright now?" he asked.

"Yeah," I said slowly.

"Of course we are." He snarled soundlessly. "Where'd you get that knife?" The hummingbird knife was sitting beside the gun on the table, beside the trivet, all casual as condiments. I supposed he would try and steal it. He seemed that way, a cur slinking around for anything to snatch. I told him that my friend had given it to me.

It was quickly I decided that he would know nothing or at least very little about me. Busily I was trying to set up a new thread of life. It was separate from the old thread—one that had been, with his appearance, snipped. For who could forgive a daughter who had done what I had. In preserving this man's ignorance there was no need for self-forgiveness. I sipped my water across from him. I felt in a new way monstrous. I looked at this man and I wondered what would become of me.

"Come on over here," Haw said. "Help me with this and then I'll make us some dinner." I looked out the dirty window to the land. This man was working on something. "Hey," he said, calling me like a dog. "Hey." I looked up, back at him. He had a ladder under one arm and a cardboard box with some jangly hardware under the other. "Let's go."

I didn't want to obey him but I did, following him out back. The wind was blowing across the outer wall of the cabin. The woods beyond were water-darkened, cold and glistening. He slammed the ladder against the gutter and it shuddered, splayed out to a semistable position. Its feet belched into the wet ground. "Now hold it there and there," he pointed. I gripped my fists around the gritty ribbed metal and held fast. I could feel my chest and shoulder pulsing painfully, endured it.

The man did not provide any commentary on the state of the roof or the visible reasons it might be leaking. Rather he made soft hums and every once in a while made a diagnostic knock or huddled down to see the roof flush. "Yeah," he said under his breath, as the colder wind pushed its way past my overalls and into the core of anything in my body that had ever felt warmth. "Mmmhmm." There were no noises in the trees. I was aware that if he wanted to kill me—with his long sugar-rope limbs, and his blady disposition—there was not a person could stop him. I felt sticky and delicate as pudding skin.

But then I remembered I could kill him too, given surprise or a hefty-enough desire. In my old life the only person I'd ever imagined killing was myself: a thought experiment, a stripe of escape.

As Haw stretched upward to begin the repair there was revealed, between his beat-up dungarees and his thermal shirt, a strip of skin pale and downy. I found I wanted to touch it. Though I was not reaching outward, toward it, I found I was imagining in vivid and close-up detail my nicked fingertip discovering this soft place to land. This isn't symbolic, but rather an image of possible intimacies.

"Girl," he broke in. "You deaf?"

I said I wasn't and passed him up his hammer. His jeer broke me out of my risky mood. Fuck him, I thought. Like a teenager I thought this. Fuck him, fuck him, fuck him. I began to think of things falling down. I had so recently been looking up. "You got that screwdriver? I need to pry this to fix it, looks like."

I plucked a screwdriver and passed it up too. Thingy sprang out the back door and wound around my legs before investigating the perimeter of the outhouse.

"Standard'd be better than a Phillips," Haw said with a light, mean snicker.

I'd never called myself a handyman, nor fixed much of anything at all. I took the one that was flat and passed it up and replaced the Phillips alongside the other jangly metal shit. "Here!" I said too loudly, and started to think about what would happen if I took both hands off the ladder, let it fall.

Instead I put my hand back on the ladder and I held it with whitening knuckles till he was done. Thingy meowed at the margins, then disappeared back up front. When Haw came down, he said "Thanks," and did a weird thing, which was that he kissed me where the side of my face met my ear. He smelled like leeching chemicals, or the landfill on a windy day. Or did I imagine this?

"No problem," I said. Though of course it was one.

THAT FIRST NIGHT he made us a canned stew he'd brought with him I imagine. It was brown but did not smell brown. Rather, its odor was some colorless burp. I gave my portion to the cat who began to sup directly.

"You like it that much?" He laughed.

"What do you have against this cat?" I asked.

"It just doesn't make any sense to me, having a pet like that up here in the middle of nowhere."

He stooped to grab at the cat and picked up its hindquarters. Thingy suffered this admirably though it was in the middle of dining. "What's up with this?" he said, pointing to the wound, whose stitches were now translucently abutted by new pink skin.

"Found it like that," I said. "Put it down."

Haw obeyed and went back to eating. "Gnarly," he said, after a moment.

"You grow up with pets?" I asked him.

He shook his head, his curls flipping. What a haggard Shirley Temple!

While watching him gather the dinner dishes, I began to let myself understand that I was attracted to him. I was no sex maniac. Rather, I was a sex alarmist: It was only the alarm that turned me on.

I wondered what he thought of me. I had been going about in Earl John's overalls, cold but pleasurably risky. I was serviceably covered, but only just, and only if I didn't move one way or the other. I did wonder what Gene would've said of my indelicacy.

Haw cleared his throat from where he was standing by the stove. "I figure I'll take the bunk in the back, if that's okay with you," he said. "You can have the sofa. Fire just got fed so it should be more cozy."

I nodded and let him hustle on back. In the heap I found a shirt and underwear and no pants, and put the damp overalls in the corner. Mercifully I discovered some blankets, too, gorged with indoor heat. In these I wrapped myself and got down into the sofa's creases. I slept quickly and hard and all at once.

Some time later in a thick dark I awoke and saw the hummingbird knife and the gun, still set on the table side by side in a faint glint of moonlight. I was surprised Haw hadn't taken the gun with him to bed, saw he didn't consider me a threat. When I shifted the sofa springs groaned low and the Thing nestled down around my legs.

There was now a new protective warmth I was feeling for this little animal. It felt important to recognize and stay attentive to this feeling, especially with an interloper like Haw in the mix. I got up and put some fresh water in a dish and put it down on the floor. Thingy approached and drank intently.

I began to stare then at the gun and the knife, which on their surfaces sucked up the thin moonlight coming through the front windows. Pretty, I thought to myself, and with my thumb emptied the magazine, letting bullets loll in arcs across the table. Then I picked up both the pistol and knife, and went back to sleep with one in each hand. Returned, I was trafficking in something new.

I WOKE THE next morning with Haw standing over me. "Hi," he said.

"Hi." It was morning and everything was light. I had, it appeared, been snuggling with the two weapons like teddies.

"You gonna shoot anyone today?" he asked, and smiled like a crook.

"Are you?"

"Wasn't planning on it."

"Shucks."

"You were looking forward to it?"

"I was."

"Well."

"Yeah, well."

"So what do you want to do instead?"

"Do?" I wanted to sleep. I was drunk on exhaustion. I was fighting my way to the surface.

"You're a real livewire, huh?" He snorted and so I sat up

and looked around, in what I felt was an exaggerated, comic way. He ignored me; I wondered why I'd tried to make a sight gag so early in our acquaintance, or ever. "You want some tea or some shit?" he asked. "We're out of coffee."

"Yeah," I said, and put the knife and gun on the floor beside the sofa, then wrapped my hips in the blanket. Soon he brought me the tea. I held the mug, which steamed. "What are you doing here?" he asked. I noticed that at some point, when I had not been paying attention, he had put the knife and the gun back on the kitchen table. They would stay there for a while, bullets astride.

"Hanging out," I said.

"You know what I mean." I was still waking up and so it was my turn to shrug. "What does a girl do to end up in the woods?"

"I don't know," I said, and went to drink some tea, only it burned my lips.

"It's hot," he said.

"Yeah, I noticed."

"See, for example, I'm here because I don't have anything better to do. I mean, look at me." I didn't know what he meant, but I looked at him anyway. His nose was sharp and beaky, his eyes hooded and green and wide set. "You get born with this," he said. "And then what?"

"You do what you can, I imagine." I was for a second flattened by his self-aware candor; I took another run at the tea, which was still too hot. I admit: I was interested in a man who used his homeliness to excuse his poor life decisions. It seemed like a clever interpretation of Western beauty standards, but perhaps that old inside-the-Beltway/college-speak didn't belong in my new life. I tried the tea again and singed my lips, yelped unseemly.

"Don't burn yourself or anything."

"I won't." And put the mug on the floor beside me.

"Wanna go walking?" he asked.

"Gimme a second to wake up," I said. "Is it cold out?"

"Not too."

"Oh," I said. "That's too bad. I'm looking forward to winter."

"You'll have to wait, if you even last it," he sighed.

I looked up at him. "You spend a lot of time on mountains?"

"No. Sometimes." He exhaled tightly. "So do you wanna go walking?"

"Yeah, I do," I said. "But not too long. My feet are kinda fucked right now." I was aware of mirroring his speech. "And my ribs or something."

He looked at me like he was making an inventory. "You were really up there during that storm?"

"Uh huh."

"How'd you manage to climb? Takes a lot of upper body strength—"

"Ropes," I said. I picked the mug up and found the tea had cooled slightly, enough.

"Ropes?"

"Yep."

"I like a girl who knows her ropes," he said, and winked

at me. Winks are the currency of the overconfident, I find. See: overwinking Hill, the garter snake edition of the copperhead now here in front of me. Still, I felt myself flushing and turned my face. He made no further comment on this, but said: "You get yourself ready. Then we'll go walking."

Haw disappeared into the back again. I wondered if my other abandoned clothes were back there too. For another moment I sat there, drinking the tea, finishing the tea, watching the shifting light of the fire reflected through the stove vents, the Thing sleeping in the flame's glaze.

Then I looked out the window, to see one branch still dressed in sweetly green leaves, on a tree otherwise brown. This filled me begrudgingly with a notion of hope. I guess it felt religious in a small and remote way. How funny, I thought to myself. What a surprise. I thought maybe this was me finally having my own life in the nick of time, here at what had so recently seemed like the end of things. Did I wonder if Pop was already dead? No, but there was a small packet of darkness in my chest which I could not reach with any near thought. Or, I didn't try.

Unfolding from the couch I got up, holding the blanket around me, and crossed the little front room—once my own little front room—and listened to the boards creak with my progress. I poked my head around the half wall and saw Haw undressed, stretching in the light coming through the back door's gaps. Looking at his body there were clear demarcations of bone structure and muscles; his butt was flat, smooth and unembarrassed: a young grown ass. "I think my pants are in here." My voice was flat too.

Haw nodded to another pile in the corner. "Go on ahead," he said, making eye contact. My skin chilled itself. I crossed the room and turned my head only when I got to the pile, fished out a fresh shirt and a pair of pants, a sweater, two mismatching woolen socks. It took me longer than I wanted it to, all the while feeling him regarding me. Like I was the naked one.

"Thanks," I said. I went back to the front room to get dressed, no longer molested by his open stare.

Soon, dressed yet no more respectable, we walked into the woods. It was warmer that day. We walked for a long time without discussing where we were going. I ventured it was north, but then east. I remembered the map in the tower, how close and far we were from anything. My feet complained without a word. We went on and on and I wondered if there was a destination or if we would go on walking as my blisters burst and then built callouses and, moving this way, we might reproduce, our offspring gestating in my uterus and then delivered, and carried, until they themselves could walk, and we, multiplying this way, might go on walking, in this snarl of a forest made impressionist by aimlessness and fatigue and motion, for goddamn ever.

So, yes: I was surprised when out from a thick stand of evergreens my lake revealed itself, surprising me for the second time in two days. Still it was like encountering a friend unexpectedly. I arranged my body to greet it: The lake's edges were silent, motionless. The water looked thick and still as a bowl of syrup. The water level has reduced slightly, I thought. No: we had come at it from an entirely different direction, and I could see on the far shore the little failing pier, just a few dense shadows in the distance. If only, all the rest of my life, I could rediscover this lake, over and over, and within this ritual discover also an endless, deepening knowing. It seemed possible. I was getting soft on the mountain, or softening from ossified.

"You been here?" Haw asked. I nodded and mm-hmmed. "You follow the creek up?" I shook my head. "We can do that sometime when your feet feel better. It's a nice walk. There's caves." I felt sickly flattered he'd thought of my feet, and a future time, all in one sentence. We weren't looking at each other, just at all the great outdoors. I wondered if I was supposed to fall in love with him and learn empathy at last. I wondered what was *supposed to* in the absence of an organizing power.

"Hey," Haw said softly from his throat's base. "Hey hey hey hey hey."

I turned to look at him, standing beside a tree. He had his cock out. Though I did not address it directly. I wondered if I should feel threatened or turned on or surprised. I felt none of these things.

Could I feel love right then? No. Though I felt we could please each other. I wanted for a sort of violence, its sweet edge. I assumed he was up for it. I did not say anything but looked out at the lake and willed the surface to move, to eddy, to wave. It didn't.

By doing and saying nothing, I made Haw think of this moment as a challenge or a game. It was soft, his cock, a less game appendage, but as he tugged it turned rigid, its finger of flesh rising against gravity courtesy of what they call a cremaster. As I watched the cock, and the man working so peacefully, so intently, on it, I remembered myself floating in the lake, my body suspended, the busy flies, the warm fall. I wanted to swim!

"You have no idea," Haw said low. I had no idea what I had no idea about. He was smiling and shaking his head like his mouth was full of a secret.

As he advanced I began to bargain with my body, who could hardly remember me in any erotic way. Hello, I said to it. You must remember what to do. It has not been so long since you were in a condo, being advanced upon, and accepting. You have done this and you can do it again if you'd like to. My body decided why not.

Still I felt a little weak and so lodged myself against the nearest trunk. In my ears were the sounds of rousing bugs, the infinitesimal mutters of wilderness. His mouth opened and he was in front of me, his car accident teeth presenting themselves. Did I feel his warmth? Did I want it?

Before kissing me he put his hands around my waist and touched his forehead to mine. Somewhere against my thigh—another island, approachable only by boat—I felt his erection. That some could feel the hardness of their desire, that others settled for spuma at their legs' nexus, an ooze from inside. How unfair! I wished for hardening in excitement. My muscles flexed in response. His body had a savory smell.

Haw paused, as we touched head to head, and asked me was this okay. Consent in the age of self-annihilation. When I nodded his head went up and down with mine. Then we kissed so suddenly I was sure I could feel my teeth chip.

From there I barely moved and by the time I did my pants

were at my ankles binding them. Haw told me to turn around. As I turned I looked at the pine trunk with its elephant skin, the spots of sap, the smoothness where a twig had once long ago been divorced, a knot also. With a broad hand he pushed me down so that I was bent ninety degrees. I took a low branch with my left hand, palmed the trunk with the other. "You wanted this," he breathed, not unkindly. I questioned myself silently and found that I agreed.

As he pushed into me it was rough and remote, and went on like that, every in-stroke until my body got used to the idea. I could feel it at the base of my spine, his pressures and work. My ribs sparked with minor pain. "How come you're such a slut?" he asked. "Just giving it up for anyone."

"Huh," I breathed, unsure how to play along, with not enough wind to form a word. I could see what he might think, from the outside of this—I did capitulate and welcome quick. "I do what I want," I lied with a new excitement. Or perhaps in that moment it was true.

"Yeah," he said. "Take it, slut." The way he said it wasn't mean. He moved his hands around my ass, palming every inch, territorial. Did I like it? I liked it enough to stay put, to see where it was going. His voice was far away and then very close, as he bent over to my ear and then bucked away. I turned but couldn't see him, only his middle third, my hips, his pelvis in bristle-curls. His balls played a vaudeville tune on my thighs. Haw asked, "You like that, huh?"

I grunted in response and pushed back into him at the right and wrong times.

We both got there, it is worth saying.

So much so that at the end of it I found it difficult to let go of the tree. "Hey," he said gently from behind. "You okay?"

"Yeah," I said, breathless and at last straightening. "That was nice."

"You're good to look at, even how banged up you are."

I stepped out of my boots and pants, and pulled my socks from my tender toes. I removed my sweater and shirt and looked back at Haw only once as I walked up to the lake's edge. "Water's gonna be really fucking cold!" he called from behind me. "Probably too cold for you."

I considered my lake. Nothing moved in the water, the tall grasses shuffling themselves confidentially. Then I didn't want to get wet anymore. So instead on the shore I squatted and peed, watched the urine rivulet into the marshy lake, waited for my own body to stop pulsing. Then I rose. The sun had gotten high while we'd been out. I wondered how much time I'd lost. There was a hawk or vulture on a far tree, a robin on a near one. Just like a girl, I wondered if we'd do it again, and how soon.

I came back to shore and saw Haw examining me. "You're real tore up, huh?"

I said I didn't know what he meant.

"You look like you've been in a bar fight. Look at you!"

I obeyed, looking down at my own body. He was right. But my body was not the issue, or an issue, really. I had used it. I can afford to use it up now, I thought. I felt I was waning. It was not that there was any clear threat: Now that we'd been around one another enough I didn't think Haw, when bored with my body, would kill me. Rather I no longer had any sense of the future, of anything that came after this, who I was now, and where, in this banged-up condition. Prior there had been that vague notion of a lonely glow in a small cabin: only me until I expired.

I had a continental map of black-and-blues across my hips and thighs, banged up arms with a few sinister-looking scabs; I found I could feel my nose peeling. The crisp air emboldened each infirmity.

"You eat anything lately?" he asked. I shrugged. "You're even skinnier than me." He wouldn't stop evaluating. By this I was miffed.

"Finally," I said. There have been times in my life that my body has subordinated my mind, and times in my life when my mind has subordinated my body, and still other times when I remember when we are one and the same. "Goal weight."

Haw shook his head. He didn't think the joke was funny. "Don't worry. I like skinny girls," he said. "But then again I like any girl'll have me." His grin was tender and awful.

With that gallantry it was time to redress and so I did, and as I did, Haw asked me did I want to keep walking after all and I said sure but after a while I said maybe I was a little tired and a little hungry and a little cold so we turned and went back the way we'd come.

On the way back, into our silence, Haw inserted the following riddle: "Two moms and two daughters walk into a store and each get one thing. When they leave the store, they got three items. How do you explain that?"

I watched a flock of birds v'ing themselves across the sky, sighed, and said: "It's a grandmother, a mother, and her kid."

With that Haw stopped walking and turned to face me. "Wow you just didn't even hesitate, did you?"

"It was clear, I feel." And shrugged.

"Well you may feel that way but it ain't that clear to most folks." Then, can you believe it, he hugged me. His arms pressed my head to his chest. I hated it, let it happen, then went on walking wordlessly. I wondered what else was clear to me that wasn't clear to others. Then I stopped wondering.

I LET LIFE go on like this, days and nights in and near the cabin with the Thing and Haw. Days and days like this. The land dried out. So did I. Often you find a punishment when you're in need of one.

On a day I'd been doing nothing at all but organizing and folding my meager, dirty possessions into neat piles, Haw came in shirtless with a full trash bag dangling from his fist. "Trash day," he said. "We have to burn it."

"I know," I said, though by that time I'd forgotten Earl John's direction.

"Come on." He gestured me out front to the fire circle in which there were a few logs. They were scaly with burn scars and I stood there until I realized he was staring at me. I was in my regular mountain clothes, fully covered in jeans and a long-sleeved shirt, but, well, a hunter knows what an animal looks like under its fur. He asked me to fetch some logs from inside and I did, the end of that dry pile I had moved what, years ago. No. Weeks.

"These are the last two," I called toward Haw's crashing in the near thicket. I let the new logs crash onto the old logs. They craned there, then found their seat.

Haw came back with kindling, and was holding a small bottle. "Gasoline," he said when he saw I was looking at it. He shook out some of the gasoline on the kindling and it smelled like civilization. Did I remember what it was like to drive? He took a match from a little tin in his pocket and walked toward me. Taking one hand, he slid it down to my groin, and pulled back the flap of my jeans. I thought he might try and fuck me right there, but he didn't. Instead he swiped the match across my fly. It lit. I giggled, much to my own button-mouthed chagrin. "I've got tricks," he said, "you haven't even seen yet."

"Don't doubt it." I pursed my lips. The match went out.

"Here, you try it." He held out a match and peeled back his own fly.

With a tentative grace I flipped my wrist across his zipper and it caught.

"Like a pro," he said. "Like a goddamn pro." He smiled with his crooked teeth and watched the match go out again. He snatched another from the tin. "One more time."

This time I moved forward carefully and as I did he pressed his pelvis forward. I looked up with my pursed mouth. "Just having a little fun."

I struck it again and cupped the flame and stepped gingerly

over to the fire circle and dropped the flame in. The fire belched and bloomed. "Thatta girl."

"I feel like you're making fun of me half the time, when you're not making a come on."

"You're not wrong," he said, and dumped the trash piece by piece—food wrappers and TP tubes, packaging and paper. I still can't say what we were doing to each other, there. Except fucking, and using each other as poor mirrors.

"Shouldn't we be doing this in a can or drum or something?" I sat back on the porch and watched him work.

"This works well enough." He looked at me. "You don't."

I stuck out my tongue and was fine with my throne. "You come up here a lot?"

"A couple times when I was younger, when my mom was trying to make me like EJ."

"You don't like him?" I found it difficult to believe that anyone would find Earl John hard to like. Though I imagined most hated Haw.

"Course I do."

"So what do you mean?"

"I guess I didn't like Lorne—that's his kid—but that wasn't Lorne's fault. Kid's weird."

"What do you mean?" I felt meaning coming.

"Doesn't matter," he said, and kept working. The meaning dissolved into the trash smoke and I began to cough.

"Go on inside. I'll see you there in a while."

"Don't you like my company?" I flirted. But I was also starting to chart my safety in and out of his presence.

He snuffed guttural, and straightened, tilting his chin. "Too much, most likely."

"Oh, brother," I said. And went inside to continue with my piles.

Later Haw came in, smelling like woodsmoke. "Gonna get this shit off me," he said, and disappeared into the back. I got up and filled a pot of water and stoked the stove and began to make soup. I could hear the splatter of the shower, such a companionable noise. I had questions in my head with no need to answer them. In this way, I was the same as I'd always been: I understood the world was more powerful than my little flesh-push self.

In a little while Haw came out naked and shining wetly. I surveyed him: his long body and the small hairs I could see, backlit with the stove's glow. His dick was a shellfish on the pillow of his balls. He had a pimple on his ass, whitish yellow with a head, ringed with pink. My first intimate impulse was to walk over there to him and pop it, but I didn't. What I said was, "You hungry?"

"Not for soup," he smiled.

"I'm not interested right now," I said, and went and got some mugs and spoons.

SOON BOREDOM BEGAN to set in. Days were mammoth and endless; one day felt like five; four days and we'd discovered a rancid brand of domestic partnership. We ate silently and spoke only in bursts. I felt that through my choice in questions— wanting to know about his jobs, his family, what he'd been like as a kid—I'd either be exposing myself or giving him the impression that I cared in a manner I did not. So I continued to refrain from asking questions. He did not kill time with his mouth either. We lived in an orderly manner, thriving in minor urgencies of intimacy. I swept and fed the cat and sat on the sofa with one wilderness book or another in my lap, unreading. I began to wonder when he would leave. When Thingy and I could resume our romantic procession into uncomplicated decay.

One day Haw was out in the yard splitting firewood and I was washing dishes with Thing beside me on the counter batting at bugs. I had been thinking of nothing but dishes, and the gunk on them, using my fingernails to chip what the water could not. I was not thinking of Ma, the large wet spot on her front, standing in the kitchen back home. Was not wondering where she was, and in what condition.

A great holler cut through the cabin. I dropped the dish I had been washing and rushed out front.

"Fuck!" Haw was standing by the stump with a long torn hole in the thigh of his dungarees.

"What happened?" I jogged closer.

"I was moving the logs and I guess something got caught—"

I was close now, and could see a long blade of a splinter breaking the skin of his pale thigh. It was seven inches, eight: a real whopper. "Here, sit down," I ordered, and led him, hopping, to the porch steps. With a ginger shimmy he removed his jeans.

I could see he was setting his jaw against any further

expression of pain. I recognized this close-mouthed desire like a brother. His breath was fast and even.

I told him to stay put and I went in and got the self-same needle with which I had sewn up the cat. I sanitized it in the stove fire and when I came back out crouched over him.

The wound was beading blood along its margins. I saw the wood under a few layers of translucent skin. Dipping my head to its level I saw it there as if submerged under a surface of water, a puddle, a pond. The skin above it was sprouted with long fine hair. "This isn't going to be comfortable," I said. "You want a pain reliever?"

"Not unless you've got some whiskey."

I shook my head. "Wanna bullet to bite?"

"Is that even a real thing?" Haw said through his closed teeth.

"Okay," I said. "I'm going to work the needle around the perimeter and try and pry the thing loose."

"Enough foreplay." He was a miserable animal.

I got on with it, working the needle along the first edge of the splinter, into the skin at a low angle. Haw's breaths grew snarly, notched, forced. I remembered the prone old man in the mall, his arms moving like combines. The cushion the color of a stormy sea. More blood beaded to the surface. Ma crying in the car. A slow rise to the surface. Haw yelped. "You need me to stop a moment?"

"Yeah," he said, shaking out his arms. A black bird with a greasy head alighted on the porch railing, and he addressed it, choked: "Get!" It flew off.

"You ready?" I asked after a moment.

"Do it. And don't stop even if I ask you to."

So I went back to work, until I had moved the needle along the entire edge of the thing. I tried seesawing it, then, under the rim of the wood. It wouldn't budge. I began to worry I would snap the needle in half. "You have pliers anywhere?"

"You've gotta be kidding me."

I could see tears pooling at the corners of his eyes. I reminded myself that this was not sadness, only a human reaction to pain stimulus. I had no interest in letting empathy pass my garden gate. I explained simply: "The needle will break if I force it more."

"Yeah. It's under my bed."

I told him I'd be back. I'd forgotten Earl John's cardboard box of tools, the ones Haw had used for the roof, and felt in his proprietary recall a sting. I wondered if coming Haw had known he'd find a young female renter, wondered if he did this a lot. There were more explanations—conspiratorial, cruel—regarding this scenario but I escorted them all out. Wide context was no longer noteworthy to me. I saw only the hands in front of my own face.

The back of the cabin smelled of the deep earth funk of a human living. Or it smelled like a place where people lived and didn't care to clean. The tarp hung from the ceiling as a provisional divider, vestigial and filthy and blue. I remembered how I had fled this place. Haw's shirts and underwear laid about in miniature topography. I kicked the box from under the bed, and in it, beside the hammer and the screwdrivers, a handsaw and a couple wrenches and nails and the pliers, I saw the gun. "Hello," I said to it. "Long time no see." I picked it up, and checked the clip, saw Haw had reloaded it. I thought about taking it back. Ideated Gene standing beside me, saying: "Girlie, a person's got to protect herself! If she has any hope of a pleasant life on Earth." This was just me: I was undesiring of any pleasantry. I was simmering.

The gun felt like I remembered: part toy, or the tail of a wild animal. A shiver went through my body, but I did not put it down. I picked up the pliers with my other hand and stood, kicked the box back under, left his hovel.

Back in the front room I put the gun on the table, next to the hummingbird knife, where it had sat that first day of my return. Salt and pepper, salt and pepper. I had a feeling of sinking, and then buoying. I stuck the head of the pliers in the stove flame and watched it glow hot, then put it under the sink faucet and let the water cool. It steamed, spat.

When I returned to the porch, Haw was hunched over his lap, his curls shuddering slightly back and forth. "This is a motherfucker," he said.

I said I agreed, then set back to work. Once I had moved the tooth of the pliers along the needle's path, I began to pry until there was space enough between the raw pink wound and wood, a quarter inch or so. Then I closed the pliers and began to pull in a smoothly confident motion. After a moment of stubbornness the wood gave up and Haw yawped open throated, cursing. Thingy strolled by like a rich man stepping over a wretch. I smirked.

"It's done," I said. We watched his thigh as blood rushed to the surface of the wound. "You need some bandages?"

"I'll just use a T-shirt, tie it around."

"Won't it get infected?"

"It'll be fine," he said quickly. He looked eager to get his grubby hands back on the wheel. I wondered how quickly an infection could move. I wondered would I see it yellow and weep. His breathing returned to normal as we sat there and then Haw looked like he was going to say something, like "thank you," like "I owe you one," but I did not want him to say anything so I ended the moment by asking: "When do you think you'll leave?"

"When do you?" Haw asked back.

"I'm paid up," I said, standing. "I told you." And left him sitting there with his long wound, so I could go and clean the back bunk as if wanting to remove not only the splinter but also his every trace.

IT WAS NOT until my body was otherwise occupied—by Haw and these related activities—that I started to grow suspicious of my circumstance on the mountain. I began a habit of holding the Thing like a baby, letting it pad at my face, smelling its rank paws. Haw wrinkled his nose when I held the cat like this. I allowed the man to dislike me however he wanted, and continued to have sex with him. I accepted that the mountain was not what it had been, did not feel as I'd hoped it would, would not again be a kooky if delusional setting of frolic and splash.

I did not believe I was doing—in any manner or

decision—*well*. I was not on the mountain to find a true love or even any companion. I knew this. Yet we took to sleeping beside one another in the bunk, Haw and I. There were no tenderships, no extracurricular pets.

One afternoon I was coming back from the purple outhouse when I found Haw standing on the porch with a question mark face. He held an old rope in his hands. A T-shirt was tied around his leg wound and he looked more like Mick than before, accessorized with his own vain folly. When I got closer he laughed as if at a private joke. "What do you want?" I asked. I knew.

"Come here," he said.

I stood where I was, digging a rut in the dirt with the toe of my shoe.

"Come here," he said again.

The air was dry and thickened by leaf mold. We stood staring at each other. I had no current intention of rope play. I stood where I was. Haw was made to condescend from the porch and grab me. Once he was close I could smell his stewed breath. It did not make me run.

"Do I have to take what I want?" he asked. I giggled and he slapped my cheek. "I guess so," he said, in a theatrical manner, and pushed me down—first I was crouching, then on my knees, then flat on my butt, until at last I was just lying faceup in the dirt, all so he could straddle me and then hold my hands above my head. The plans men have. My breath was constricted by his weight. I was not being trespassed upon. He was merely performing on my stage.

As Haw began to wind the rope around my wrists I attempted to make of the moment some levity. "You do this a lot?" I asked. He didn't answer me, was focused on his task. The rope was tight but not painful. "How's your thigh?" Again he didn't answer. His clothes smelled of woodsmoke, and beneath, a pickled odor from his pits. The veins in his arms erected firm pulsing ridges, riled.

"What will you do to me next?" I asked blankly. I was wondering if Gene might show up in this, my hour of embarrassing not-need. That would teach me. "Denise," I imagined him saying. "It's time to skedaddle!" I admit this daydream proposition lightened me, made me glow.

"Don't be such a brat," Haw said. I began laughing again and couldn't stop. Haw's determination brittled. I could tell by the way his hands relinquished their grip, the way his posture straightened. "Dude," he said sociably. "I thought you said you liked ropes. Are you not into this?"

You're a jester, and not a villain, is what I thought then.

Before I could negotiate, or even say a word, there was a fomenting in the brush: a scratching and snapping of branches and the intimate puffs of flora rubbed against flora. Immediately Haw stood. I rolled to my side and used my elbow to sit up, hands still bound.

"What is it?" I asked. "Can you see?"

Haw shook his head without looking back. The crashing seemed to follow a pattern of crash, crash, wisp, wisp, crash. It was not scary sounding, though I knew: any question posed by wildness could be answered by some new bodily harm. When

I had at last gotten vertical, I stared where Haw stared: at a knotty bush, naked of leaves, from which emerged a toddling skunk.

We stayed in place. I don't know if I had ever seen a skunk prior. Their spray had been on the wind sometimes, while Ken and I drove late in the more rural parts of the county. But here are the skunks I had put my eyes on, up until this point: cartoons. See: Pepé Le Pew, the long-suffering, fuzzy-on-consent Looney Tunes lothario. Full stop.

This animal was the traditional black-and-white, with a plume of a tail, a diamond-shaped skull, a small perturbed snout. I could have hugged it, for its lack of menace. Though my hands were bound and my judgment sharper than dull.

As we watched, the Thing emerged from the brush behind, low to the ground in a gorgeous stalking pose, shoulder blades peaked and moving tidally under its fur. I had never seen Thingy look so wild. The skunk seemed uninterested in the cat, who continued to switchback just beyond the swipe of that plumed tail. I was aware that the cat was about to be sprayed; I was aware that in remaining inactive I was allowing something I loved to be in some manner harmed or driven to discomfort; I blamed the rope binding my hands, and I blamed Haw too, but blandly.

We watched a pattern emerge: the Thing would rustle up its strength to pounce. Then the skunk would turn to greet it. With this confrontation, the Thing would sweep backward, play it cool. Then the skunk would continue its amble, its tail bobbing *hello, hello*. The Thing would resume its liquid stalk, its green eyes professional in their attention. The two animals progressed across the width of the clearing this way; what were they doing but waltzing; what were they but about-to-crash cars.

For on the fifth or sixth lap, the skunk presented its asshole and let go. Poor Thingy turned tail and surged into the woods. The smell, I should note, was a multiplication of the dankest weed times the rottenest egg: In it I shuddered.

Then, I said to Haw: "Get this fucking rope off me." He did as he was told, rope ends whipping as he untied. Once freed I went off through the skunk-smelling thicket to find the Thing. The cat was cowering at the foot of a tree, beneath a bush, in the approximate place we had so recently found ourselves advanced upon by this interloper, Haw. That'd been just about a week prior—each day having remade the terms of life on the mountain, of self-removal. I scooped up the cat and promptly vomited, still holding on.

When I came back to the cabin clearing I told Haw to go get one of the empty plastic tubs and put it on the porch and after he did these things I put the Thing in it gently and told it to stay put and went inside to get some peace from the stink. At this Haw rolled his eyes.

"It's not like we have any tomato juice," I rued through the open door, looking around the mess of the cabin.

"Yeah," Haw said. "But we do have plenty wood ash."

"Wood ash?"

"What, did you grow up in a city?" And then, again, that crooked smile of his, that greasy scythe. I watched him cross to the ash bucket and scoop a bowlful. I wondered was he playing a prank. He didn't like the cat, and the cat didn't like him. But the stench, catching in my every crevice, outstripped my caution.

"Bring 'em here," he ordered, standing in the kitchen.

I went out and fetched the Thing in the tub. The cat squirmed and yowled as I conveyed it. I wondered how aware it was of its sorry state. It did bat its own nose.

"Now put it on the table." I did as I was told, and watched as Haw bent over into the tub and began to rub the ash into its coat. At first the cat froze but then started to lean into Haw's massage.

"You're such a slut," I said to it. "Giving it up to anyone." Though I did not like myself when I said this.

Haw continued to massage the ash into the Thing's fur. His confidence in this made me sure he had grown up with animals, though he'd earlier denied it. He went on rubbing the cat with the ash. The stench eased up.

When Haw was all done, he washed his hands in the sink and told me, "Put it out." At first I didn't know what he meant, but then I saw he meant the cat.

"How come? Doesn't even smell anymore."

"Does so. It'll teach it," Haw said.

I consented as if hypnotized, transported the cat by its trunk, let it down on the porch to lick and spit. I remembered, then, once lying down on a stranger's bed, the thick silver frame on the nightstand, the plastic sucking at my thighs. Under Pop's novelty hypnosis, in that empty and stale house, I wondered if I had learned to obey or simply to tolerate, surviving.

Only one other time had Pop taken me to an empty house. Between the first two cancers, I had gotten sick at school. The hallways had gone liquid. I sweated and dripped and could not follow the story of the day as I usually could. I sat in history, heated. My nose whistled grievously. "Lettuce leaf," Gene'd whispered in my ear. I hocked. "For godsakes let us leave! Before we're flooded out!" The teacher continued her lecture about the Defenestrations of Prague. I did not laugh with everyone else at the idea of someone launched from a window, so knew how sick I must be.

"Are you okay?" Ken asked from his nearby seat. I shrugged miserably, put my hood up. Later I would learn that what I thought was a cold was walking pneumonia. I requested reprieve with a hall pass. In the health room the nurse asked did I want to call my folks. I did. Ma was then working as an assistant at the library. Pop was working too, but available, with full agency and rosy cheeks. I imagine he thought he was going to keep living, and then die much later, as an old man. A mistake of duration only.

When the Toyota arrived I laid across its back seat, letting the seatbelt buckle dig into my hip, closing my eyes. It was January, just after break, and ice crystals constellated on the window glass. "You okay, sweetheart?" Pop asked. I said I was fine, and just needed to rest. It was unusual for anyone in the family to admit noncancer illness; as someone else might say: The goalpost had been moved. He told me we just had to swing by one of his properties. I asked him why, looking up into the rearview.

The mirror showed his eyes and brows and a hairline holding fast and lush into his fifties. He told me the last time he'd shown the place he'd been sure there was something crawling in the master bedroom walls. A squirrel or raccoon. He wanted to check again before calling the professional.

"Will they use a have-a-heart?" I asked, for as a teen I was still occasionally sentimental.

He said he didn't know, but hoped so. A nice lie. He parked. "Do you want to come in?" I said no but he said I should, that it was too cold for a sick girl to stay put.

"Four bedrooms, two and a half baths, a finished basement, an old hot tub any new owner will chuck," Pop said, as he opened the lockbox and unlocked the door. I sat on the grand foyer stairs, sniffling, and listened to Pop's steps fade down the upper hall. This house was vacant of stuff, static with anonymity. Soon Pop came down the stairs to report: definitely something in there. He drove me home, then, and sent me to bed.

Later Pop would report that it had been a squirrel, that they'd gotten it out. I'd ask again about the have-a-heart. "Denny," he'd said. "We're all just doing best we can." He was a seller and a shower and spent no sentiment on such things.

I could tell you that this story is how I first set my eyes on the house Ken and I would break into, the house from which my hummingbird knife would be claimed. I wonder about my impulse to identify nonexistent-but-possible coincidences. It's a desperate habit of making meaning. In analysis it's embarrassing.

But it was not the same house, merely a big house one neighborhood over in the other direction. This was a story about a squirrel in the wall, on the occasion of a skunked cat, in which there are no coincidences or doppelgangers. It's only time and impulse that summon its meaning, if any.

All night, post-skunk, while Haw snored horribly, poor Thingy cried outside. The serrated yowls bored into me. I had not heard such sounds from the cat, since—well, since I'd shot it. But I had shot it and then healed it, lost it and then found it. I was not in favor of this Haw-heralded disruption. I'd sat up till Haw walked into the front room, eyes in heavy slits, to ask would I sleep next to him. I consented, though I understood the decision as a betrayal.

All night I watched Haw's nose hairs flatten under the force of his inhalations. My mouth tasted sour or bitter. I felt myself to be a low-down creep and stayed awake listening, punishing myself this way. I had wronged my last and only friend. That's the last time I'll do that, I thought to myself. Of course I'd never have another friend, up here. I'd see to it; it was safer that way.

When the sun began to rise I got up and let the lovely animal in. Its little pink nose was smudged with ash. I scooped the Thing up and addressed it: "Hello," I said slowly. "Will you ever forgive me?" A trace of the putrid skunk scent draped still. "Oh honey," I cooed, sounding like someone I didn't know. By gosh I was indeed getting softer.

Thingy twisted from my embrace and walked back out the front door and arranged itself on the porch, squinting with some kind of accusation I was probably imagining. "I'm sorry," I called to it. I did want to cry, only my body was not capable of doing so. I did not deserve any cooling release.

Haw emerged from the back. "Who're you talking to?" he asked. I didn't answer him, only stood where I was for as long as I wanted to. He didn't come any closer.

•

LATER THAT MORNING Haw had oatmeal going on the stove. As we sat at the table to eat, the Thing came in and jumped up on the table, winding itself around our bowls. "Get!" he said, and pushed poor Thingy down onto the floor. It skittered into the far corner of the front room. Bits of ash still clung to its coat.

"Don't hurt it!" I yelled, too loudly. This was the smallest gesture that might be expected: Minimum was my specialty.

"It's not hurt," he said, rolling his eyes. His chewing made a private, wet noise. "I thought we could go up to the caves today."

I shrugged and said okay, still sore at him. Sore for the cat and not for the rope burns. The sex was fine or even pleasantly annihilating. This was not enough or worth it really, this human complication in my animal life.

But I did want to see the caves. If this were to be my mountain, my dwelling or planet, I wanted to inspect its insides also. I was hoping that at some point the man would leave me be and I could be mountaintop queen, reigning sovereign, or at least dead. After I cleared the breakfast dishes and Haw went out back to shit, we dressed.

The gun and the hummingbird knife were still next to each other on the table. Haw took the gun and loaded the magazine. When he saw me looking at him, he said, "In case mountain lions."

I had not seen any mountain lions, the skunk being the largest animal I'd encountered—but I still nodded and then took the hummingbird knife and pocketed it. He looked at me. "For defense," I said. Once, in green sociability, I'd asked a man

whether he'd ever tried a salt lick. Now, I carried a knife because I might need to use it.

"I'm all the defense you need," Haw said, hooking the electric lantern to his belt loop.

I ignored him and walked out of the cabin, flip and mean
and sassy. I was getting impatient with this rank incursion. He
followed, muttering.

We crossed the meadow and shimmied along the far perimeter of the lake until we came to its tributary, a creek no
wider than a driveway. Haw limped slightly. "This sucks," he
complained of his leg.

"Baby," I said meanly.

He didn't complain again.

As we worked upward along the water, it constricted, ran
deeper, made elegant noises of rush and fuzz. I saw a crayfish
skimming the water's edge, some small fish in the deep, and two
blue herons sewing a crooked hem along the sky. Farther out,
a hawk, or so Haw said. "Or maybe an eagle." For an hour or
two or three we worked our way up in clear natural silence, the
cat following along like a companionable shadow. Soon we were
the highest I'd been since settling in the woods.

Haw stopped. "We're here," he announced. From the high
vantage in the thin air I could see clearly the lookout tower on
the horizon. Before us there was a long flat rock that looked for-
mal as a banquet table in its proportion. Above it was the brief
remaining balance of the mountain peak, and I wanted up. But
Haw said, "Come on." I trotted along like I was his bitch but
this was a performance built for ease. I was pretty sure I'd get

back and do some housecleaning, by which I mean I was pretty sure I'd take the cat and hit the road, drop out somewhere fresh.

Beneath the rock table was an opening about three feet tall and four feet wide and horizontally we shimmied through it: Haw first, then me. The Thing stayed outside, pouncing at flying bugs it couldn't catch. Once we got inside I saw how the cave opened up, until even Haw could stand with just a little ducking. A few feet more and the cave began to constrict again, into complete darkness. He set the lantern at the cave mouth. There were the low noises of the river water: a trickling, tickling piano.

"This all fills up in heavy storms," he said. "Would hate to get caught in here." I had, all over again, that tricky feeling like he was going to do me harm, bind me with ropes, leave me here to drown. I tried to decide if I would care. He began to kiss my neck.

As I pressed closer to him I could feel a hardness at his hip which was not his cock. I wondered how many empty beer cans he'd shot, how many squirrels. Here I believed I was happy for the gun to be out of my custody.

He got real close to me then, put his face astride my jaw, and licked his tongue up the length of my face. "Baby," he said. Perhaps we would go on spitting the word back and forth into one another's mouths. He didn't know me at all, but why should he.

In tandem we undid our flies. He pushed his pants down over the knotted T-shirt and took mine off and shucked them into the cave's damp. He lifted me onto a shallow ledge and kissed and kissed my neck, whispering: "Baby, baby." As he entered or lodged I felt myself tighten. "Baby," he said. I watched the bright mouth of the cave as he began to thrust; the Thing had stuck its head into the opening and was watching.

"Baby," he kept saying. The Thing was now wriggling through the cave mouth, its whole lissome brown furred body, and I thought, as Haw worked his way in and out, that I had never seen a more beautiful creature than this little cat. We went along this way, the three of us—Haw and I in our unholy congress, sweating and dirty, the cat investigating gently at the edges—until I felt Haw move in a different way, his hand down at his thigh.

The gun was out, loaded. The gesture had started. The shot ripped out a blue echo, which surrounded us. I felt gelded, then enraged. He was still inside me. "It dead?" I asked, breathless. I didn't want to look.

"Yeah," he said.

And so presently I rose and set upon him, throwing the gun into the far darkness. It clattered and I renewed my advance. For I was wiry with all this time on the mountain, and my skin was one big bruise. Pain can feel like immortality. I slammed his shoulder into rock. He pushed me back up. We were well matched, similar weights, both of us rangy and strong. First one of us had the upper hand, and then the other; it went back and forth like this for quite some time.

"Get the fuck off me," he snapped, but at the same time had his hands digging into my flesh. He hoisted me into the air and let go. I fell hard into the water, my bare tailbone hitting rock. Reports of this bounced around the cave.

We began to wrestle down in the cold water, our warm

blood splattering across rock and skin. The gravel and pebbles and dirt embedded themselves in every wound.

And at the hot center of this fight, when I could barely breathe, I noted that there had been a distinct lack of confrontation in my life. It's almost biblical, isn't it? How I, toasted so gently in the oven of the suburbs, was forced to climb a mountain in order to see a conflagration with my own eyes?

At first it seemed like Haw would beat me down; to tell you the truth I thought I was beat, the way he'd thrown me. But he was meaner than he was smart. As I scrapped for footing he was still down there in the water, distracted by the aftershocking pain of my elbow having dug into his concave chest.

I dropped my full weight atop him from as great a height as I could manage. Then I yoked my arm around his neck. Then I spit in his face, and the spit included a tooth and blood and a great deal of dark energy that I was at last ready to let go. I had him pinned and I did think about picking up his sorry skull by the curls and hitting it against the rock bed until it was time to say goodnight. We were locked together in a fearsome jigsaw way.

"Let me go," he said. Straddling his chest I dug the hummingbird knife out of my pocket and whipped it open, pressed the blade with a steady light pressure on his Adam's apple. Its rainbow wash shone.

I looked down to see Haw, to see Rip Van Winkle, I mean, Mr. Hackett, I mean, that painting, I mean, Gene, I mean, Haw: a man who was being haunted by himself as far as I could tell.

"Let me go," he said, quietly.

I thumb-rubbed the hilt of the hummingbird knife up and down. The only best part of death is that it happens to everyone. Then I drew away the knife and folded it. I pressed where I knew the splinter had been, right on the knot of the shirt. "You fucker!" he screamed. I stood to my height and looked down at this pitiful stranger. His eyes were scared and widening, as though straining to see my great new proportion.

Haw got up and began to back away from me and this movement was like a tonic to me. "Hey you crazy bitch," he spat.

"What?" I replied to my apt and lovely moniker.

It was perhaps the cast of my eyes, their lack of sex or softness, that taunted him. "Who even are you?" he asked, unspooling his limbs loose and bleeding into the air around him. I stayed buttoned and staunch. "Hey you crazy baby," he said, moving closer. We were both still working to catch our breath. I wondered if he was ready for another round. I held the knife in my fist. "Hey you crazy, crazy baby." His mouth was swelling and curdled.

I charged him blindly, so quick he could do nothing but fall.

He didn't say anything after that. I sucked my body away, and never touched his skin again. I moved apart from our arena. I looked back to see a darker splotch beneath his head where he lay face up. He had fallen on an outcropping of rock. I had or had not made this happen. I did not look at him again. He could be dead or alive. He could still be dead or alive.

I thought: Maybe now he won't have to worry about infection.

There at the opening of the cave lay my cat's body and I did not look as I dragged myself out of the cave and waded, naked from the waist down, into the deepest part of the deep part of the creek, letting the cold water nick away all the dirt. The pain came bright and loud and the weather, this autumn day, was clear and gorgeous. I was drawing myself up and out, awake, at last alone on the mountainside, no man or cat or imaginary gent to disrupt the busied noise of the forest—my dumb flopping heart, a secret within it. The secret was that no matter what I did, I was alive, and one day I'd die.

I ran or stumbled downward, semiblind, in a liquidating blur of green and brown and dark brown and gray, attempting to follow the water. When I hit the lake I swam across for no reason but my body wanting it. The water was warmer than its tributary, amniotic, thick with plant life. I swam in a sloppy freestyle stroke with my head above the water, then scaled the dock and sprinted across the meadow. I wanted to be far and farther from the cave and its contents. I believe I would have kept going, all the way down the mountain and into some town, had it not been for the pain which, every few minutes, issued news of injury.

My intestines were their own continent of horrible. Upon hitting the cabin clearing, I loosed myself in the purple outhouse and then walked up to the back door and knocked shave-and-a-haircut. A show for a lonely gal. I mean a gal alone.

I waited for no answer. I opened the door. I crawled inside and got on the back bottom bunk in the people smell and lay there, surrounded by Haw's castoff clothes, looking up at the roof, its raft patch, the blue tarp. Later it rained briefly and when it did, the roof began to leak once more. Each leaking drip sent me deeper into misery. In the pain—which ran along my limbs and throbbed heartily from nose on out to skull—I was alone. No cat, no pal, no enemy. It is an only child's burden: to have the feeling of deep solitude husbanded by parental psychic noise. And now here I was, not a child. Just an only.

At some indeterminable point, my pain fell beneath my need to piss and eat. That evening, I pushed myself vertical and squatted in the shower cube. While doing so I saw on its wall a small blot of old cat blood on the vinyl, and shook.

On top of this I got my period. As if my innards wanted to be clean and forceful for this new version of life. I washed all of my bodily issuances into the drain and then washed myself.

The prospect of fresh air felt like a threat. For each time I shifted, my skin opened up at a different scabbing wound: I bled. I dripped and ached and smarted. Where? Oh, everywhere.

After dressing in the front room, I looked at my old piles of stuff. I found the tampons, a sign of comfort and preservation sent by my past self. Everything was cruel and possible. I ate in maintenance. I chewed in a daze. I consumed bars and nuts and anything I didn't have to cook. My hunger was endless and I tried to meet it but it rushed away to deeper and deeper crannies of my gut. I sighed, and knew it was time to leave. My first idea was to crawl gingerly up the creek, find the caves once more, and then die.

But you must by now know this: I am a bending branch who'd sooner snap than rot in place. So I—drinking water and pissing in the cube, trying to forget my endless hunger and pain—decided that I would sleep again, well as I could, and then go out and try and find some people to help me. I was weak and added weakness to my idea of self.

This time I lay on the couch. Everything in the cabin was dusty and dirty and smoky and skunky. I was disgusted and ashamed, and it was only with the last bit of a pain pill, found in the gutter of a pants pocket, that I was able to greet sleep.

IN THE MORNING I dressed slowly and went out into the world. It was cold but not upsettingly so. The deciduous trees were dull yellow, or flame red, or brown and sloughy. The evergreens were darker. I dragged my body in between their trunks, all day, until I hit a hiking path. There I leant up against a tree. I wanted to be dined upon by some animals: What better penance could I offer to the world? I did not and do not believe in a higher organization of the cosmos. And still I asked an ant if it was interested in my flesh. It went on crawling by. "Didn't get her when she was a pup," I remembered Gene saying. "But I still trained her." Then—unbit, in solitude—I slept in place, pinned by my fatigue.

IT WAS A half day later or more, when two trail custodians found me there. They wanted to call the Rangers. I begged them not to, said I could walk, said I was fine, if they could just give me a ride down-mountain.

Later they transferred me from the trail vehicle to the truck, where I sat between the skinny one and the fat one such that

my knees were touching theirs as we bounced down the provisional road. The skinny one talked, but I didn't listen. The
fat one hummed quietly. When we got to the visitors center, he
helped me out. "You got anyone to call?" the skinny one asked.
I nodded and recited Earl John's number without thinking why.

Once we got to the visitors center, I used the restroom and
jerry-rigged a pad with toilet paper. I'd left the tampons in the
cabin. My inner thighs were covered lightly in my blood. My
period was thin as a crick and would end soon after. As if my
body were now doing only what was needed, no more. I avoided
the mirror.

Later a chatty woman fetched me in her hatchback and
drove down-mountain. She was the wife of the skinny man or
the fat one, and a nurse practitioner, so asked me should she take
a look and see how I was doing. A Christmas tree air freshener,
pineapple scented and the color of a Post-it, swung from the
rearview jolly. I said no thanks. She gave me a clean sweatshirt
with the name of a corporation on it. I watched the mountain
trees cede to broad roads and low houses. She made a turn onto
a dirt road where a double-wide, a prefab shed, and a garage
stood together across from an open field. "Here we are," she
said. As if that meant anything.

When we rolled up the gravel drive, I saw that Earl John
was out front wrapping his plants in burlap. A warm bath of a
sigh pressed through me.

"I know honey, it'll be cramped, but they keep a nice house.
I was there last Easter and EJ made a great corned beef you
wouldn't turn down." I did not like her though she had done

me a great favor. She waved at him and stopped the car and I got out and she backed the car back onto the dirt road and drove away.

"Hi," I said.

"Hi," he said, and led me into the house.

The woman from the outfitter was doing the bills at the kitchen table, wearing reading glasses. As we entered, she finished a jot before looking up. "Nice to meet you proper," Janey said, and waved with her hand, which was dry looking and small. Looking at her face I could see now the wide-set eyes, the landscape cheekbones. Planes of faces built by the same genes. She was petite, though. A whip of a woman in flannel, corduroy. A splinter in the world. I shuddered privately.

She put the bills away. We sat down together. They got me a beer and a plate of pizza bites and a dish of Bugles and I ate them quickly, lucky not to choke. I told them then about the tree falling on the roof, said I'd gotten lost in the woods trying to get off the mountain. In minor ways the story was true. Did they ask questions? Only if the latrine was still standing. I said yes; Earl John nodded to himself.

I said if they didn't mind I could sleep the night on the couch and start for home the next day.

"Well of course it's your decision and I've got your truck in the garage but I don't think you should head out so fast," he said.

"No, you should stay here and rest a couple days, call someone to come up here," Janey said.

I said yes I would call someone, but I did not then call

anyone. My body reminded me of its weakness. I needed to rest and would do so poorly. I did not ask any questions, then, did not ask anything a person in my situation might want to know, but later I gathered from conversation that Janey was indeed Haw's mother and that Haw usually came and went as he pleased. Though I worried he no longer did anything, that he had never left the cave, that he was a carryout snack for any creature who happened by. I did not, did I, blame myself; I did not, did I, sleep very well: up all hours still and watchful in this warm strangers' place. The trailer was faux wood paneled in a honey color and the rug that ran through it was an orange shag. Like being in a safe flame.

EACH MORNING EARL JOHN would ask how I was doing. Each morning I would say that I was doing better. Each morning I would be lying. He'd go out to his woodshop and out on errands and wherever else. "Going to the cabin?" I'd ask in an overly light manner. No, he'd say. Wanna get you squared away first.

For most of this duration I slept in the days, huddled in Janey's recliner opposite a space heater. Earl John, every once in a while, would come in from the shop and rouse me with some soup or hot Ovaltine. I wondered if he still had the jigsaw his wife had been so good with. I wondered if his nerdy son had found some off-line friends. I took showers, and shivered wetly afterward, dressing tightly in Janey's spare sweats. Winter was closer. The old man did not ask after my supposed art. Looking back, I can't explain why he was so kind to me. I suspected Janey had some ideas about where her son had recently been.

And when I was alone, sometimes I wondered if Haw, alive, would crop up like a bad penny. And Gene did seem gone for good, but who knew. Undeniably I was vulnerable to such bedevilments. The trailer door looked like it was made of steel, and I tried to let this comfort me. At night I sweated into the couch, thinking about how thin the boundary was between my abdicating heart and the busy world. There was a window above the couch, by my head. Its glass chattered in the frame. Often I'd wake to hear a bird's caw and startle down to my gut.

What did I think of myself, as I watched Janey move about her home, watched her leave each morning scrubbed for the store, and return each evening muzzy at the edges? I worried my empty dental socket with the tip of my tongue. I had the runs; I pressed on my injuries; I would not—though she offered several times—allow her to dress my wounds with ointment and bandages. I did this myself, even as it was twisting or awkward to do so.

After four days my body was feeling a bit better and my mind was clearing and I had logic-summoned the reminder that, dead or alive, Haw was no great prize. In fact he was, I believed, a dangerous man. I wondered whether his father had been dangerous to others or just to himself. I resisted any collection of information regarding Haw, only watched the trailer's lamplight lick his mama's face, the pitted complexion transforming into a clarity of hospitable warmth, as she knitted or did Sudoku, sitting there in her recliner. I could leave. He would never find me. I've found in this absence a rare mercy.

Soon I was well enough to help Janey or Earl John with dinner, chopping cucumbers for the salad and setting the table like a teen. One night after dinner I asked them if I could use the phone. "It's long distance," I apologized.

"Honey, everything's long distance from here," Janey said, and went and fetched the cordless.

As the phone trilled my chest hurt. I realized I was holding my breath. I pushed myself. I thought: one day, madam, you'll strangle at the gates of your own closed mouth. Then I inhaled. Swept the overgrown feeling from my eyes. Ken answered.

"Hello," he said.

"Hey, Ken." I bent my voice submissive and soft.

"Well, shit," he said.

"Hi," I said.

He asked where the fuck I'd been. He said that he'd told my folks I was fine, on a trip without a phone. He'd told them: she needs space, a break, give her a little time and she'll be back home lickety-split. Pop had said, Can you blame her? They had made a story for me. I had so many terrible faces.

But meantime Ken knew how lost I'd been. I felt sorry that he'd been alone in this. But I didn't say so. Instead I asked: "Think you can take the bus here and help me drive home?" Like a peach, no hesitation, he said he would. Said he could take the bus soon as Saturday and come and meet me. I was ripely embarrassed. We hung up and I felt myself make a single puff of a sob. My body was a high-pressure system. A storm I wouldn't let break.

•

TWO DAYS LATER Earl John went down to fetch Ken from the station. While I waited for their arrival I decided to take a shower. The thought of the water calmed me. Some things don't change. I was just done dressing when Ken came through the door. He looked like himself, tidy and whole next to tattered old me. He hugged me from behind, my shoulders in his armpits, cooping me with his long solid limbs. I was a lizard sunning itself on a hot rock, to be in such a hug; again I did not cry, this time in joy, but thought of it. I pressed my chin into Ken's arm. We hadn't said hello.

"How long was I gone?" I asked Ken finally, twisting my neck to look up.

"Month and a half," he said. Something I noticed then but did not comment on was the fact that he had finally fixed his broken eyetooth.

Forty-five days: I took this duration into what my future would feel like. Some things happen quickly, then nothing happens for a long time. I would have to get used to this human hurry-up, this human slow-down, for once more I seemed to have a future. "Anything happen while I've been gone?" I swallowed a sandy breath.

"He's still around," he said.

I tried to read his face but it was shut for the season. So I unknotted myself from Ken's embrace and gathered my belongings: my thin wallet, my keys from Earl John's hook, my hummingbird knife, one sweater which I put on. I left my jeans, shredded to shit, and that corporate sweatshirt. Janey, appearing from the kitchen, informed me I could "wear the sweatpants out." I thanked her heartily and loudly, for I could be no churl-ish troglodyte, anymore.

Ken followed me outside and we stood in the driveway with Earl John and Janey. On the other side of the road was the long inert pasture, its grass cut down to the quick. Its sight depressed me. "Take care of yourself," Janey said. Grimly I nodded my chin all the way to my chest. Then I thanked them again, and apologized belatedly about the state of the cabin.

"Ain't no thing," Earl John said, somewhat merrily. "We've had bikers up there, seen worse."

"It's pretty bad," I said.

"We'll slide my son a couple bucks to go straighten it up," Janey said, like a mother would.

I thought then that I had been wrong about her understand-ing of my state and its cause. I thought, what if Haw was alive and paid to clean the old abode. I thought of this possibility: Haw drudging his broken body all over the cabin, our atrocious mess. But then I thought of this probability: Thingy up there in the cave, or, Thingy's body, nibbled and nested and consumed by animals small and large. I exhaled, and smiled slightly, and looked back over to the field, its blank bristle. My neck muscles released their crimps.

BEFORE I REALIZED it, Ken and I were on the open road, sitting beside one another, quietly, silently, as the world washed by us. He petted my shoulder, one hand on the wheel. He smelled of chemicals, or of chemical fragrance, that note of city living. I breathed it in, felt pleased, fell asleep.

Throughout the trip I'd wake to watch the landscape, to see the man-made marks, then fall asleep again. We traveled on, across one or two state borders. We did not, as I had, take the country roads, but rather: a long series of interlocking highways wide and beckoning for use. Signs assured us of direction and distance. I slept.

When I woke again the truck was stationary, in a gas station next to a Super 8 Motel. It was dark. I got out and saw Ken, through the wide window of the mart, turned away from me. Still his movements struck me like family. I walked to the building. I went in.

In this fluorescent light box I felt part taxidermy. But otherwise I was not notable. There was a man in a cap with his back to me, surveying magazines, and Ken was standing in the chips aisle with no apparent understanding of his predicament. The slushie machine and the hot dog carousel together made a cozy harmony. The taquitos shivered, rolled. Everything around me looked equally ridiculous and sincere. I wondered if Ken would notice me, or if anyone would, here, or in any public. I walked the aisles of food bags with the other unnotables. Were we all really drooling, or was this simply what it felt like to be back in a peopled landscape? I felt ornery, gooey, itchy, sinister. I tucked my knife away into my pocket. I followed Ken to the candies, made my presence known.

"You woke up," he said.

"That's true." I had a sudden clawing hunger, and picked up a king-sized bag of chocolate-covered peanuts. "Can you cover me?"

Ken said he could. This felt kind, if remote, so I took more advantage and asked: "Did you tell them anything else?"

He said: "That seems like your job."

"Don't you want to know what happened up there?"

"Not really."

I did wish otherwise; withholding's less profound when no one's asking you to give. "Do you think they'll be angry at me?"

"No."

"Why not?" I ripped open the bag of candy and began to pour it down my gullet, then offered it to Ken while I waited for him to answer. It tasted like, what, motor oil mixed with confectioner's sugar and pebbles. Had my biomechanics wilded? No. Maybe I was just actually paying attention.

He cut his eyes sharp. "I told Dan, 'Your daughter loves you. Even if she's not here.'"

"Ouch," I said. And meant it precisely, for it was an injury scooped and pangy. The man in the cap walked between us and we divided then re-adhered.

"You can not care," Ken said. "And that's a fine way to be. But you can't not care and care at the same time."

"I can," I said as he walked toward the register.

He got a pack of Marlboro Lights and added, "Those," waving back at me. I held up the candies. Then I poured them out on the ground, followed him out to the music of their skitter and roll.

When we got back in the car, Ken didn't turn the ignition key directly. "I'll be better to you," he said. "But you're going to have to wait." Like a kid I wanted to ask, "How much longer?"

Instead I bounced my head, looked out into traffic, said I understood. We went the rest of the way home.

I WAYFARED INTO my own old life. I had to relearn convenience. Alone I sat in the bath or on the toilet and felt four starred. In the mornings there was a moldy frost across the lawn. In the mornings there was wheat toast, heavily buttered, with a knife on the butter plate in case I wanted more.

I found for the first days I wanted mostly to stay in bed and not be bothered. I parked the pickup on the street and left it there. It was selfish to set the limits of my own days yet I could not rouse. Though by the second or third week there would come a new and vigorous balance within me. Then I would brightly escort my father into his last days, as my mother approved from the margins.

But first: Ma marched me to her GP. The doc pronounced me "banged up but, overall, fine." This felt accurate to all of us. In the dentist's waiting room I watched videos of porpoises set to sunny instrumental plonks; later they recommended an implant and I promised one day I'd take the time. Until then I'd be fine to chew on the one side.

In my absence, little had changed. Well that's not true. Pop was less of a body, or less embodied. I was never sure which. I did recon slowly, dawdled at the door of my parents' room, asking Pop at last: "How are you?"

"Keeping body and soul together," he said, so predictably that I mouthed along with. I knew he was no longer trying. He was in fact courting deviation. I let him do and say what he wanted without protest. It was not kid-gloves so much as a lumpish attempt at beneficence.

Occasionally there was less clarity; Pop would drop one line of talk and divert to something else, or silence. He'd ask a vague question, then drift during requests for further detail. It was like walking into an empty building, where you'd expected to meet someone.

Meanwhile, Ma seemed to have achieved her most high maternity, sans neurosis, sans frizzle: no *try*, all *do*. The house was neat, the surfaces markless. Ma washed produce three times and stuck to organic. The meals were nutritious, smelling thickly of protein. Pop ate less than he would have liked to, and I ate as much as I could, and Ma preferred snacks to meals but yet she piled all of our plates.

Carmen the hospice nurse came three times a week and, later, five. She wore bright scrubs and most days, an amethyst pendant. She was highly trained and quiet, or, merely low speaking and professionally calm; she'd been there all along. When she talked we didn't have to and we liked her for it. She liked us because we never interfered with her plans of care. She talked to the doctors, and administered meds when working. From her we learned to try and be simultaneously honest and gentle. Belatedly we learned to nest. We made popsicles. We bought soft blankets. We settled in.

For now Pop was alive. This was the headline. Now I felt— if not ready, then closer to. I would perform my duties when needed. I lived there in the home alongside my parents. I waited to see if either would address me regarding my absence. Once, weeks in, Pop cleared his throat during the interstitial musical swell of an also-ran flick about mixed-up wartime lovers, and said, "We're glad you're back."

What choice did Ma and Pop have but to forgive me my disappearance, now that I was back and behaving? Ma was grateful that Pop would see me, his only child, prior to his expiration. Pop was grateful I was around for Ma. I was transistor and diversion both. With my decaying dad, I made jokes about other people's bucket lists: around-the-world trips and cruises and skydiving and the opera. "I'm afraid my tux is at the drycleaner's." Pop looked at me like I was his reflection, then laughed.

Meanwhile I wondered if Gene would ever come back. I'd wake in the night beneath the comforters in the orderly one-door room of my childhood, and stare hard into the dark. Sometimes I'd whisper: "Who eats floating fish but flies?" No one took the bait. Not one bite. For this I thanked myself.

We made it through the winter, in the hummy buzz of neighborly visits and holiday television specials. We watched movies. We played cards: war, hearts, gin. Was there ever a waiting room more comfortable than life. We leased a wheelchair for Pop, and sometimes wheeled him around in it.

ONE DAY IN May Carmen was off. The house squeaked with disinfectant. Our rooms were shot through with new spring light. I hardly recognized us. Ma had been working three or four days a week, but she was off too. On the way to see if Pop needed anything I walked by Ma, who was standing on a kitchen chair in the front room. She brandished an extended-handle duster, yielding cobwebs. "You and he should go to the botanical gardens," she said from above. "He'd really like that." The gardens weren't very far away, an unexpectedly pretty spread back beyond an elementary school and a small housing development. They'd taken me often as a child but I'd stopped thinking of the place some time ago.

"Don't you want to come, too?" I called up.

"Nah." Her syllable spread elliptical. I wondered if the doctor had said something more precise about expectancy. Previously he had said he did not want to say, that any approximation over or under three months would be a blind bet. Now it'd been nine months, gestational in number and palliative in nature, since Pop had followed through on his decision not to pursue treatment. What I did during those months is now a smear of glasses of water and laundry soap and newspapers and errands to one strip mall or another. Soon I'd start thinking about a new job, about making contributions to the family bank and bills.

"Fine," I said. "If he wants to go we'll go."

From her perch she said I should invite Ken if I wanted. "He can help with moving Dan from the car to the wheelchair and stuff."

I said Ken was at work, which was or wasn't so. He'd been showing up for family dinners only, no extracurricular pal time. "I can do it," I said, and passed her by, on to the room where Pop still kept himself most hours.

Inside he was standing on his own power by the side of the bed. The room was no sibling of its former state. There was almost nothing in it: a clean white room with a mechanized bed.

Beside it, a comfortable chair where Ma often slept. No coin bowls. A small plastic tub in an appealing blue, containing nausea and sleeping pills. Along a shelf, military lines of Pedialyte bottles and a row of lotion-added tissue boxes. The spring light was here too: Pop had raised the blinds unevenly. They came at a slight down angle from one corner of the frame.

Pop's muscles were wasting; his bones were heavy. He stood now with one hand against the wall. "Denise, good morning!" Because I had already done the traitorous thing, and been forgiven, I could look him in the eye. For in his body's translucence, his eyes were more vivid. I smiled at him now, and meant it. This is no sap song. This is just a daughter doing her best to be un-evil to a father who could no longer stand so great. We contort endlessly, within the confines of family. I asked if he felt like going to the botanical gardens.

"Yes!" Pop said, as if charmed. "I think I forgot they existed." I said I had too.

Soon I put the wheelchair in the back of my parents' sedan. Then I helped Pop down the steps. It was hard to be slow beside him, when my muscles wanted to work. This was a most loving endurance of slowness, I said to myself. This slowness keening into stillness. Ma stood in the doorway and waved goodbye.

AT THE GARDENS I helped Pop into his chair and we moved through the greenhouse, its sticky fragrant air, past banana trees and orchids and birds-of-paradise and the cloudy tank of piranhas.

Then out to the British rose garden with its rows of

American Beauties and Golden Celebrations, the Damasks and the Sunsprites, alive with the heavy zooms of beetles, the leaves perforated in misregistered patterns. Pop didn't wear his sunglasses; he let the sun project.

We moved up the long, shallow hill past the lilacs with their bunched, boasting blooms and their sweet shoppe scent. The beauty here was not everything but it was one delight left available. I tried to remember this. We ringed the lake, cross-stitched with acid green algae. Fat-bottomed geese waddled like drunk mascots. "They're not nice," Pop said as we passed them. "Steer clear." So I did, down the path that led us into a thin woods.

"Promise me—" said Pop as we moved through the trees, but didn't finish. As of late he had said this often. I understood this as a habit of control, or its appearance. We came upon a large stump that had been cut into a kind of chair or throne, by the removal of a chunk of it. The remaining surface was smooth with skin oil and use.

As a child I'd sat there calmly. Royalty had then meant for me: security, plus power, plus self-satisfaction. In the throne I'd felt this, wanted Pop to feel this too. It was a poor equation, but I beckoned. "After all," I said, "you're a king among men." Then I winked.

Pop shrugged and said OK. I helped him, one hand at the hip and the other at the shoulder, from the path, across the mulchy forest floor, up the little hillock to the throne. No one in our family believed in any idea of heaven or reincarnation. Life was a 1 or 0 proposition. You had it but you didn't get to keep having it. The smell of the forest was not different from the smell of the mountain. I believed I could smell its colors, its bright budding greens and its brownly decaying shadows. I kept thinking the phrase: I'm ready enough. Though I didn't mean it.

I had a feeling we were then supposed to say important things. We didn't. Rather we stayed there in silence. A body beside a body, though I felt nearly alone. A wind riffled the vegetation and the geese honked overhead and the leaves waved and in all of this we were unmoving. Pop cleared his throat and asked what was next. I suggested ice cream, thought of poodles. Pop apologized that he didn't feel like it. I said, "Then let's go home."

On we went, through the forest, up past the side of the rose garden and the back of the greenhouse and into the lot and into the car. We revved up and down the neighborhood roads and the four-laners, past the churches and strip malls and dry cleaners and gas stations; on, to our smooth little road and our driveway and our house, which was ours wholly only as long as we were able to possess things, that is, as long as we were solvent and alive.

WHEN WE GOT home there was a strange car in the drive. I parked on the street and popped the trunk. We'd become used to pilgrim acquaintances dropping by to say hi and bye, before. I wondered who it'd be this time. Getting out, I wrested the chair from the trunk to the ground, unfolded it. There were strangers walking toward the stoop, a couple. I helped Pop out of the car and into the chair. We approached; they turned.

Their veins showed through their thinning skin. They were breeching elderly, had mobile mouths on the vivacious edge of grins. Today their age and disposition were ostentatious.

"We were passing by," the man hollered out at us, "and we thought we'd come visit you."

"Oh yes," Pop said like a confused host. We were working toward them, toward the stoop, and we got there by and by.

"We don't live in town anymore," the man explained. "But we were back through visiting and then we were driving past your house and I said to her, I said, 'Why not stop by and say hello to the finest real estate agent in town?'" The four of us approximated cordial guffaws.

"You sold our house and then we had to leave!" the woman said. It was meant as a joke but I could hear in it a real accusation.

At a low volume Pop said: "You bet I did!" And then: "It was my pleasure." He said he didn't do that kind of work anymore.

"D'ya miss it?" the man asked. He descended the stoop, his wife behind him, and shook Pop's hand in turn. This man was a villain for reminding Pop of his losses. These people were monsters, I felt. I imagined that I could hear their teeth shifting in their mouths.

To change the subject I began to ask them where they lived now but Pop interrupted, answering: "You give people an opportunity, selling their house, let them choose something else."

"And let's not forget about the American dream," the woman said pridefully. She wore a visor low on her forehead, and progressive lenses that obscured her eyes.

"I would never," Pop said, solemn and on the unfamiliar

rim of sarcasm. He half-smiled at me only. Here I saw his real human consciousness knocking thinly and dearly at his fading body's door. It sent a sparring shock into my heart. I set my jaw.

The old couple made moves down the drive. "Well we just wanted to say hello."

"Hello!" Pop said, overbright.

They nodded at us. Soon they were getting into their car, chatting low to one another. One of the man's sentences was picked up at the wind and thrown at us: "Gosh, he looks terrible!"

I was ready to fight them. But I turned to Pop and he was laughing. "I do!" he said. "I do look terrible!" His humor nipped at me. I helped him from the chair and up the stoop. Ma came out to help.

Let him have anything he needs, I thought to myself as I waited, hands braced, for Pop to get to the door on his own power. I blamed myself for everything but had no strength to right it. From then on I would extend to myself a nihilistic benevolence, experiment with radical blamelessness, and sometimes sleep well.

THAT NIGHT I drove to see Ken's new one-bedroom in Eastern Market, a gentrifying neighborhood where you could walk for a coffee or a drink or a bite. What a novelty after so many years in the suburbs. The apartment was fine: new appliances, wall-to-wall carpet, white walls. "Yeah," I said.

We sat down on the sectional, which was also new, and nubby. I told him about the couple. He shrugged. "Isn't it nice that people care?" He knew that it wasn't.

"No," I said. "It's not nice."

Then later, while we flipped channels, he said: "I'll get over this. Don't worry. I love you."

And I said back: "Is there any more beer?"

There was more beer, and we tipped it down our gullets, swallowing noisily. The walls of the apartment were undecorated. I put my head on Ken's chest and he laid his hand on the side of my face. Sirens and headlights flashed through the windows onto the back wall. There was a commercial for detergent. There was a commercial for soda. My ear against his sternum, I could hear his heart beating: a pleasant hassle. There was a commercial for cat food. I woke in the middle of the night and exited, like I always did. I checked the knob to make sure the front door locked on its own.

BEFORE POP DIED, on a spring Sunday afternoon, there were plates of broiled chicken breasts, steamed string beans, and oven-baked potatoes addressed with butter. Ma had *transcended*, or that was the word I thought, each time I looked at her in her well-moisturized face. I wondered whether my absence had goosed this new decorum. We ate the chicken in a meditative manner, grinding the strings of meat between our molars, letting the butter lubricate the potatoes' dry starch. I admired our dinner, chewed around my empty socket. I was, in some way, at peace. Or I thought I was; I thought again: I'm ready enough. The mantric lie, smooth as injected plastic, would take lifetimes to decompose.

After this meditative supper, and after some light stretching,

Pop wanted to go out. "I'm going for a drive," he told us. I woke from a nap on the front room couch at this announcement, let my vision focus to his features: smiling and gracefully gaunt, looking like history. As he jangled his keys, I roused myself upward and joined Ma, who had come in from the kitchen, coffee in hand. With hydraulic elegance she let the mug down on the counter. It made no noise. What I'm saying is that she'd found a new couth. Pop said again how he wanted to go out, and alone.

He wanted to see the earth and the neighborhood and to bask in the season. He hoped he would see more lilacs. He wanted to see the houses and the people in houses, the people living their lives. He wore a polo shirt and a sweater and a barn coat, for he was always cold in those last days. He wore his woolen slippers and adjusted the belt on his oldest jeans and stood in front of us like a hero departing for a long and resolving journey. Then, he wanted a hug.

What can I say but that we had a family hug, the three of us embraced into one object of genetic matter, of organic matter, degrading into one another as all families do, provided they are proximate or as claustrophobically nuclear as we.

Pop left the house, walking slowly. He did not want the chair. I napped. Ma straightened objects in the home.

POP GOT IN the car, and spent extra time simply sitting in it, feeling the old-friend leather of the driver's seat, tracing an index along the wheel. He was disinvested in earthly things by now, he thought, but still found very much to be beautiful—pleasurable, even—and opened the windows to let the air in.

He pulled out of the driveway carefully, looking both ways, checking his mirrors twice and then a third time. There was a minibus stopped up the block and he waited as it discharged passengers. There was a brood of children and the children were all acting caricatures of emotion: one ecstatic, another in theatrical head-down sadness. He felt okay. It was slightly shocking to feel okay. Nearly neutral, at peace. Or, he wouldn't call it peace; the vein of fear in him was too wide. What he'd once felt was anger, but he no longer let that through the door.

When the bus continued on, so did he. For a while he was behind it, watching the children return to their houses, doors pressing in to their privacies. The lilacs were indeed there in clusters and heavenly, sending their almost-rot scent through the open windows and prompting Pop to sigh.

He made a left on the next street and saw a woman walking a very old dog, and he wondered why they had never gotten one. Perhaps, after he was gone, his wife would get some mutt. For Ma, for Marilyn he wished this, and for me, his daughter? Likely some kind of settlement, a smoothness and responsibility to my days, to come before the consent of my own expiration. The evening light was pink, and every piece of siding reflected this tone. So much of this pink, this interior color. In it, Pop felt expansive.

He directed the car, then, down a narrow, unpaved cut-through, which ran along a small creek. He wanted to look at the wildflowers that grew by the water, and to sit on the bank or imagine doing so, imagine feeling the wet softness of the ground through the seat of his pants. The creek's bluff shore was six feet high. The family had, only once or twice, picnicked here. He regretted that it had not been more. Then he let go of that.

He shifted to *park* and sat calmly in the car, by the creek. He looked at the skin-thin petals of the blooms, and did something close to meditating—breathing slowly while smelling the mineral and the mud and the vegetal green, for quite some time, and then longer.

Grinning with this, his mind carbonated with old joy and new delicacy, Pop set his foot on the pedal and started the engine and put it in gear. He was very far from his body, somehow, and the distance was only increasing. He was, what, a dry leaf on a true and relentless wind. The vibration of the car, and the stream trickle, and kids somewhere shouting, and music from a stereo somewhere in the middle distance—

The car lurched and pitched down the little bluff, into the shallow water, and lastly as the car began to roll he realized he was going the wrong way, quickly, only it was the right way, as any way would have been. The car rolled until it was upside down.

Sometimes when I think of how Pop said bye I think that it was overly convenient, that it was a merciful gesture I did not earn or deserve in any fashion. But then there's this: he was still dead. His consciousness was over. We all live knowing of this regular and unavoidable loss.

The next week we sat in a law office in the presence of a respectfully glum stranger. His left French cuff had a grease stain; I watched this as he made the posthumous report. Who needed glamor, I thought, in times like these, or ever?

Pop did not, it turned out, want to be buried, as he and Ma had discussed during the kidney issues of yore. This was fine with Ma; he wanted to be cremated. But the second part of the demand unsettled her with its witchy romance: He wanted his ashes to wait, until such time that Ma's body was also ashes, so that the ashes could be commingled. I was to do the commingling. I only wish he'd asked. And specified what to do with the resulting admixture. He professed, in the document, not to care. But I did not want to make it a permanent installation, wherever I'd be living then.

We would not, I resolved, bicker over Pop's wishes. It was unseemly. "Ma," I said lightly. "Do you care?" She reported that I could throw the ashes down the garbage disposal, as long as they were together. We laughed!

The lawyer, politely ignoring this warm family scene, drummed his fingers and reported that everything of Pop's would go to Ma. There was life insurance that would make her life slightly easier than it could have been. There were debts to settle still. The lawyer said goodbye. We said goodbye too, and passed through the low halls of the building, and out into the daylight.

KEN SLEPT OVER that entire first week, on a sleeping bag next to the sofa where I myself laid down each night. My room was available but I didn't want to go in it. Ma slept there instead. Ken seemed sorry. Or he behaved like he was sorry. Or I imagined he was sorry. I was sorry too. Some nights, we spooned. I let my body sink into his, corseted by his arm, and hoped we wouldn't topple off the couch. I wanted to talk about normal things but couldn't say the words.

DURING THAT FIRST week, tasks were completed, requested and expedited by phone, by other people's off-screen industriousness. Expressionless company men came and fetched the wheelchair, the mechanized bed. This was replaced by a new mattress and box spring, on which Ma pledged she would someday sleep. The cremation business was easily dispatched; there were, after all, professionals and their systems and templates for such a thing. I tried not to think of the oven. At the bank I arranged for a safety deposit box in which to store the ashes. It was unclear if this was legal, but I didn't care. I wanted them out of the house. Rounding a corner, talking or laughing or dusting the mantel, I did not want to encounter the ashes of my father—it would upset our work toward loss tolerance, to be reminded. We tried to make it easier for ourselves but failed. There would be no blossoming acceptance, only a kind of gross seep.

•

IN ABSENCE OF a service we held a dark and dressy open house. It was a damp affair. I don't mean the eyes: just the day, its feeling. It was unreasonably hot, summer in spring. People sweated into the folds of their mourning togs. There were tears, though not from Pop's stoic womenfolk. I stood like an ancient cairn, beside Ma, who performed a role I could not have named. She patted shoulders and let people talk to her, explain at her, though I do not think she was listening to anything, except, perhaps—if she was like me—the long and low drone of shock tearing through the otoliths and canals and cochlea, blotting out any good word, or, indeed, any word. We all go through eras of feeling and not feeling. I was in some area of my body grateful for the casseroles that came through the door. Ken stood as Pop's most proper envoy, slick and doleful in his navy button-down and dark khakis. The real estate folks raised their beer and wine, a toast for Pop, and his long-loyal family. Carmen gave us a hug, and a clutch of sunflowers tied with a white silk ribbon. The day grew long. The mourners left. Even Ken evacuated. Then it was only us two. We drank wine in the same room, and then separated to sleep.

I thought then, or understood: there is no next thing. I was no longer waiting. No anvil swinging. I lay back in my old bed, Ma in hers. Before sleep I barked a sob then shut myself off. We repeated this night many nights. Without Pop the house felt anonymous as a chain motel room in an unremarkable town. It promised nothing but its walls. I attempted not to think of Ma, hands crossed over her chest, eyes open in the imperfect dark.

•

ONE MORNING I woke and turned toward the light beyond the
blinds. I had left a half-emptied glass of wine on the sill. I rose
to take it to the kitchen sink.

Ma was at the table looking at the newspaper, some lighter
section. Home, or Style. Weekend. The pages shushed like skin
running across skin. I found I perceived many things like this,
now: of the body (gross, intimate, decaying) or not of the body
(null set).

I poured out the wine and ran the faucet. I put the glass in
the dishwasher, clicking its stem between two stanchions. The
kitchen was clean and its lack of disarray felt meaningful. However I felt unable to wonder why. Would Ma be like this forever?
It would only last the shock. I had been gone. I had been gone
and things and people were different or the same. I resisted any
wet sentimentality, any saturated animal feeling, only wanted
the sharp blade of loss. It wouldn't come; it wouldn't come for
years.

Later beside the kitchen sink I saw a tall white candle
poured into a glass cylindrical volume. I asked Ma what it
was for and had she bought it. She responded in a vague way.
"Someone left it the other day," she said. "I couldn't tell you
who." Indeed it was not a gift anyone who knew us would've
left. Who knew us, even, anymore.

My but Ma's hair looked greasy in the sunlight, clumped
at the crown, supported by a buttress of flaked scalp. We were
letting it ride, weren't we. No, we weren't—for I blinked again
and saw that her tresses were clean and arranged, and shining

as a brass doorknocker. I had simply seen what I'd been used to seeing. We were marching on. We were not so depraved as to eat, metaphorically, floating fish. We killed, metaphorically, what we ate. And kept finding ways to stay alive.

"You're supposed to burn it and keep it burning, in memory," Ma said, not looking up, with her stunning, clean hair draping the sides of her face. "You'd know things like that if I'd ever taken you to services." Not making eye contact. This was a kindness. We were now worried that everything we said would mean something. Even though nothing we ever said meant anything, not to ourselves, and not to each other, not past the obvious, not past the factually true.

"What should we do with it?" I asked. Ma got up to come look at the thing. "I guess we could burn it."

"Burn it or throw it out."

"I'm not sure I'm at the try-anything stage of grief yet," I said.

Ma clicked her tongue percussively. "I think I might be hungry."

I could not remember her ever saying this, prior. I'm certain she'd said it prior and yet. "Let's go to the diner," I said.

"No, I don't want to." She suggested pupusas. I countered with pizza.

While we considered this I watched her take a matchbook from a little dish, a round dish that double-exposed just then with the cabin's sun-shaped trivet. I had been so many places. My body was here now—a mass of things pulsing, a mess of things, a mess, a body. I watched Ma take the match and strike it, and light the candle. She set it in a bowl of water and put the bowl and candle in the empty sink. "This is how you do it," she said, seeing how I watched her. On a zipper, I thought. Cup the flame with your hand. Some gasoline—

"So pizza?" I asked.

"Okay," she said. "Yes."

We went to the strip mall and got a small pizza with green peppers and sausage and split it, with Sprites, chewing and swallowing like people do. The vinyl tablecloths were smeared with grease; the crowd was burbling genially and I didn't know what day of the week it was. Surely all around us were those who'd experienced loss, not currently thinking of it. Who had the faces of lost loved ones set in thick silver frames, on coffee tables and bedside tables and dressers. We chewed. We filled our stomachs. Ma paid the bill.

When we got home I walked directly to the sink to look at the candle. There was an inch now of molten wax, clear as water. The small flame spread its orange, reflected across the steel basin of the sink. I retreated from its burn.

We went about our day and night. We watched the local news. We did not discuss where to put the crates of tapes. We went to our separate beds. I texted Ken: "Had pizza with Marilyn. Don't worry. Talk soon. XO." He texted back: "Thinking of you. Call tomorrow."

Since all of this I have tried not to hold on to any clear intention. I left my resolve on the mountain, my anger too. But for a while, I thought daily of every death, past and potential. Then on one otherwise unremarkable day, I did not; I thought nothing of my past. Every day I wake up and the world persists. It is nearly incredible. I live by inches or acres. I am not who I was.

That next day when I woke I saw that there was a gauzy, spreading mist hanging above our overgrown lawn, over the clovers and dandelions and broadleaf dock, all shuddering in a breeze. The mist behaved as a Vaselined lens. It felt too symmetrical to my own state. I was in the mood for performative acts; I was in the mood for breakage; I let this drama push me into vigilance. I went to get a glass of water. In the kitchen sink the candle burnt on. There was the heavy transparence of liquid wax, for inches. Then a bright new translucence all the way down to a small disk, which weighted the wick at its base.

I put my hand above the flame and felt its heat. I felt the radiating heat of the glass. I felt my palm heating as it reddened and baked. When I thought I would not be able to stand this for much longer, I lowered my hand over the mouth of the candle. I sealed the volume and watched the fire go out. I recognized myself.

ACKNOWLEDGMENTS

This book was made in the context of great care given by many people. Thanks to my agent, Caroline Eisenmann at Frances Goldin Literary Agency, for her galvanizing editorial work and guidance, and to my editor, Jennifer Alton, for her trust, sharp perspective, and vision. Thanks to everyone at Counterpoint Press, for their incredible support.

Thanks to Alissa Nelson and Matthew Leach for providing me supporting information about fruit flies in a lab setting. For Denny's reference texts, I used *The Complete Wilderness Training Manual* by Hugh McManners and *The Art and Science of Taking to the Woods* by C. B. Colby and Bradford Angier. As I wrote this book, my repeat readings of Mary Ruefle's stunning piece "Monument" (from *The Most of It*, published by Wave Books) inspired my usage of the word "conflagration" and the passage surrounding, which can be found toward the end, during the final movement between Denny and Haw. That movement itself was cued by Carson McCullers's *The Ballad of the Sad Café*. Several books, films, and artworks were influential to the long process of writing this novel, but these informed it most materially.

Thanks to the generous friends who have read and talked to me about this book over the years, including but not limited to: Dani Blackman, James Scott, Elizabeth Ellen, Kyle Winkler, Diane Cook, Rebecca Rukeyser, Laura Adamczyk, Suzanne Scanlon, and Olivia Cronk.

Thanks to my wonderful mentors at the Washington University in St. Louis MFA Program. Thanks to Kathleen Finneran. Thanks to Kathryn Davis, Marshall Klimasewiski, Kellie Wells, and Kerri Webster. Thanks to the writers there.

Thanks to my friends and teachers at Hampshire College, who emboldened and inspired me. Thanks to Media Services, for the fun and for the knowledge.

Thanks to my colleagues, and especially thanks to my student writers—with whom I have learned so much—at Washington University in St. Louis, at the University of Michigan, at Eastern Michigan University, and at Northeastern Illinois University.

Thanks to the Vermont Studio Center and to the Sewanee Writers Conference for their support and community and time. Thanks to the great writers, artists, and facilitators I met at both of these places, who read and talked to me about earlier drafts of this book.

Thanks to my oldest friends, Joanna Kete Walker and Amy Knesel. Thanks to Alex Baldino. Thanks to all of my friends, for being the people they are and for doing the work they do. I am so grateful.

Thanks to the Erickson-Guss family, and thanks to the Barnes family, for their steadfast and warm camaraderie.

Thanks to the Hickses, new family I'm so, so lucky to have.

Thanks to my dear, caring, and funny uncles and aunts: David and Marty Schindler, and Susan Goldblatt and David Dean (in memory).

This book is partly dedicated to the memory of my grandmothers, Ruth Schindler and Pearl Goldblatt—both adventurers in their own fashion. I would also like to memorialize here my grandparents Oscar Schindler, Harold Goldblatt, and Elaine Goldblatt.

Thanks to my parents, Abby Schindler Goldblatt and James Goldblatt, whose immense love and support have made my life and work possible. I could not ask for more.

And thanks to Jordan Hicks, for his sweet conspiracy. His brilliance, compassion, love, and partnership have made my life, my life.

© Jordan Hicks

AMANDA GOLDBLATT is a writer and teacher living in Chicago. She was a 2018 National Endowment for the Arts Creative Writing Fellow, and her fiction and essays have appeared in such journals as *The Southern Review*, *Noon*, *Fence*, *Diagram*, *Hobart*, and *American Short Fiction*. *Hard Mouth* is her debut novel.